STRANGERS IN TREFOIL STREET

STRANGERS IN TREFOIL STREET

by Dorothy Webb

SCRIPTURE UNION
5, Wigmore Street, London, W1H OAD

by the same Author :

THE HIDE-OUT

Printed by A. McLay & Co. Ltd. Cardiff and London

I

THE first Saturday after they'd come to London the Pendray children thought they'd like to go to Regent's Park. Heather persuaded Norman and David that it was just the right day for the Zoo. They each had quite a lot of pocket money at that time. When they'd left Cornwall the Wednesday before, lots of people had come to say goodbye to their mother, and the children had come in for a good many parting gifts from old friends of their father, from kind uncles and aunts, the Pendray grandparents and so on. In fact it had been better than Christmas was likely to be. Only they didn't know about that.

When they'd got to London there'd been something of an anti-climax. The journey had been all right, but rather tiring, so that they hadn't appreciated the ride across London on the Underground as much as they would have done later on. Then there had been the electric train and then, when they were all quite weary and David (the youngest) was getting snappy, there had been the arrival at the flat.

Grandad Parker—their mother's father—had spent a lot of time searching for a flat in London, and because they were so hard to find and Mrs.

Pendray couldn't afford a high rent, this flat had been all he'd been able to get. The Pendrays, therefore, should have been very grateful, but they weren't. They all thought the flat was horrible and the trouble was Heather said so, at once.

'Crummy! We aren't going to live *here*, are we? What a dismal old dump!'

Of course the others had done their best to make amends for that remark or to cover up for it. Mrs. Pendray had said that when they'd unpacked and put some of their things around a bit she was sure it would look very nice, and Heather and David were tired and must go straight to bed. Norman had tried to change the hurt look on Grandad Parker's face by asking him if it was far to where he and Grandma Parker lived, but the answer to that had been both disappointing and surprising,

'Oh, no—only a ninepenny on the bus,' said Grandad. To Norman, that sounded like the other end of town.

The next two days weren't at all enjoyable either. They'd each wandered, bewildered, round his or her new school, rather taken aback at the noise everyone made and the fact that they couldn't understand what the other children were saying, although, of course, everyone was speaking English.

It was a relief when Saturday came—and the thought of the Zoo. Mrs. Pendray, who had very little sense of direction, said she couldn't tell them

6

which way to go but they must find out exactly where it was before they started. She didn't want them wandering off and getting lost, as London was such a big place. (She didn't know London at all herself because her parents had only come to live there after she'd married and gone to live in Cornwall.) In Cornwall the Pendrays and their friends had wandered off regularly every Saturday and had never got lost, but even they could see that things were rather different here. There was nothing you could get your bearings by—no fields, lanes, rocks, cliffs, no sandy coves. Worst of all, there was no sea—but at that time the Pendrays had not been in London long enough to miss it. London was just rows and rows of tall grey houses. Just that— street upon street of them, with an occasional rubbish-littered space, and now and again a row of poky little shops. Somewhere in among the tall grey buildings there must be something famous to use as a landmark, but they didn't know how they were going to start looking for it. The Pendrays knew already from their experience of going to and from school how easy it would be to get lost in such surroundings.

Mrs. Pendray said she couldn't come with them to the Zoo because she still had lots of things to unpack and sort out, and as the children hadn't a map of London between them they all trooped down the three flights of stairs to the front door-step to sit down out of their mother's way, and decide what could be done.

It was there they spotted Tony and decided he was a likely person to ask. He was clearly local. He was sitting on the edge of the pavement, bouncing a football in an absentminded way and blowing enormous pink bubbles out of the gum in his mouth. Norman went across to speak to him.

'Excuse me,' he said politely.

He was rather astonished at the result. Tony jumped to his feet, clutching the football under one arm, clicked his heels together and made a tremendously extravagant bow, and then said, 'Deloited O'im shooer'—or something that sounded like that.

Norman didn't know what to say for a minute. He knew Tony was making fun of his politeness, as this seemed to be the way all the boys at school behaved to him. One of them had said 'Proper posh, aincher?' on his first day and Norman was beginning to take a dim view of all Londoners. But Tony was shorter than Norman and rather fat—he called himself 'stocky'. What was more, he had that kind of round face and blue eyes generally known as 'honest'—not really the face or figure for extravagant bows.

So Norman couldn't help grinning at the sight, and this, it seemed, was the right thing to do because Tony grinned back. Norman relaxed still more.

'Can you tell us the way to Regent's Park?'

Tony scratched his short fair hair and looked puzzled.

'Regent's Park. Now I've heard of it, hang on!' He went on scratching and said 'Hang on!' three more times and screwed up his face horribly in thought. Then he stopped scratching and screwing and looked at Heather and David who'd got tired of waiting and were coming slowly across the road.

'Naoaw!' he said, 'I can't. But I can show you the way to Brixton Park.'

His offer was meant to be friendly but Norman thought he was being dim.

'No, no, *Regent's* Park we want. You know, where the Zoo is.'

Tony stared hard at him and the next thing he said seemed to Norman to be even dimmer.

'D'you come from America?'

'No, of course not.'

'It's that funny way you roll yer "r's" ' said Tony, grinning again, but in a very friendly and interested way. 'It sounds a bit like them cowboys on the telly, you know.'

Heather had been standing by listening, now she burst into peals of jeering laughter.

'What rubbish! Don't you know a Cornish accent when you hear one?'

'No need to be rude!' interrupted Norman quickly, frowning at her. Heather tended to go around saying nasty things to people and just not caring these days. He said to Tony,

'Don't take any notice of her. She's only ten.' He knew that would make Heather behave better as she hated people to treat her as if she were a kid.

'This is David,' he added, 'he's eight. They're my brother and sister by the way—I'm Norman.'

Tony's face had been getting friendly again during the introductions.

'My name's Tony—Tony Forrest,' he said, 'I'm thirteen.'

'So am I,' said Norman, feeling pleased to have found someone his own age at last. 'Look, will you come to the Zoo with us? You can show us the way then.'

Tony looked doubtful.

'There ain't no Zoo round here, I can tell you that for a start.'

Norman tried not to start arguing with him.

'London Zoo,' he said patiently, 'it's bound to be in London, isn't it? And it's in Regent's Park. All we've got to do is find out where Regent's Park is. Surely you know.'

But Tony didn't know. He kept saying he'd heard of it (but in a rather doubtful voice) and in the end they saw the postman coming along the street with the second post and they asked him. He was a nice cheerful whistling postman, but his face went rather sorry for them when he answered.

'Regent's Park? That's up North—miles and miles from here.'

'But London Zoo——'

'London's a big place, son. We're in the South West here, see, and London Zoo's in the North West, so to speak. Take you a long time and cost you a lot of money, then you'll have to pay about 4/- to get in—each of you.'

He saw their disappointed faces and added kindly, 'You could go to the Crystal Palace Park, you know, and there's a Zoo there. Not a great big one, but it's got some nice animals in it. There's an otter, I believe, and all them prehistoric animals. They're not real, of course, they're made out of stone, but you'd like it. It's about one and three on the bus.'

He had to go on with his sack then and he left them standing in a little group, with very long faces. He'd got them a bit mixed up through talking fast and in Cockney so they all thought that all the animals in Crystal Palace Zoo were made out of stone, even the otter, and they felt terribly disappointed. The 'one and three' on the bus put them off as well, they didn't realize that he'd told them the grown-up fare, and one and three was a lot of money to pay to go and see stone animals. But in any case Mrs. Pendray had said they weren't to go on buses until they knew their way around better.

In the end they all went to Brixton Park with Tony and kicked his ball about on the grass. And that was what they ended up doing almost every other Saturday all through the winter. Tony played a lot of football matches and sometimes Norman and Heather went to cheer, and sometimes Norman went alone.

Mrs. Pendray had a job in an office and had to leave the house in the morning even before the children went to school. She didn't get in till about an hour after they'd got back, and on Saturdays and Sundays she cleaned the flat and did the washing so was too tired to take them anywhere round London as they'd planned in the exciting days when they'd been looking forward to seeing all the wonderful places they'd heard about.

Heather was very disappointed about the London Zoo because she loved animals. Norman had looked forward to seeing the Sutton Hoo Burial Ship at the British Museum because he was interested in History, particularly Vikings, and David had wanted very intensely to see the axe at the Tower of London (he was a blood-thirsty boy, you see). And they all wanted to see Buckingham Palace and as many princes and princesses as happened to be around, and, of course, Trafalgar Square and Nelson's Column, the Houses of Parliament and Big Ben, and so on. They'd made a great long list, and Mrs. Pendray kept promising and promising and then putting it off because she was so tired.

Tony seemed perfectly happy to kick the football

around Brixton Park on non-match days and Sundays too. He thought Brixton Park was a delightful escape from the row of tall terraced houses that made up the street in which the children lived, Trefoil Street it was called—nobody knew why—but the stretches of green lawn in Brixton Park certainly made a delightful escape from it. The houses in Trefoil Street were very narrow and very dilapidated. They were, in fact, waiting to be pulled down, which was one of the reasons the Pendrays had been able to find a vacant flat there. The houses on the other side of the street were all empty, and their gaping windows had been jammed up with old wooden doors to prevent the street kids and the vandals from climbing in and out and stealing things. Behind the lived-in houses in Trefoil Street there was an empty space known as *The Debry* which was a very suitable name actually, only no one knew what it meant. It was a great big stony rubbish dump, with a few rusty cars and prams and bedsteads dotted here and there all over it. But mostly it was stones and bits of paper and dust.

At the far side, hiding it from the main road, were some very large advertisement hoardings, but you could only see their backs from The Debry. Even the Pendrays, who'd been used to real fields and country paths with the wonderful fresh clean air coming across from the Atlantic, began to think Brixton Park was nice after a few weeks of living in

14

Trefoil Street and looking at The Debry out of the back windows.

Heather, however, sometimes used The Debry as a Thinking Place. There was nowhere to get away and think in the flat, because it was December and very cold and they could only have the electric fire on in the living room. If Heather decided she simply had to get away from the boys and have a think, and if she went into the bedroom and jumped up and down in her coat and scarf to keep warm while thinking, then loud knockings would come up from the people in the flat below. So Heather used to go out on to The Debry and tramp about and think. It had some advantages over Brixton Park—it was quieter in some respects. There was always the traffic noise rumbling in from behind the hoardings and there was the noise of the electric trains going back and forth on the other side, but there weren't so many children there. Sometimes there would be a stray cat, gone half-savage—but they kept well away, and anyway Heather liked animals. All except dogs. She was terrified of dogs, so she always took a good look around to make sure there were none there before she ventured on to the tin cans and the litter, to think.

One day she had checked for dogs and there were none, so she was prowling back and forth, pondering. She was thinking mainly about how awful London had turned out to be and how she would like to be back in Cornwall. She was forever comparing the two places in her mind. The flat was awful, she thought, for about the thousandth time. The furniture was shabby and worn; it only had two bedrooms so she had to share mum's, and there was only a double bed and she hated double beds.

'I want a room of my own,' she thought, aiming a savage kick at a tin can. 'It's not fair! I had my own room in Cornwall.' Then she thought about her father and how he'd been killed in a car crash last spring, and how she missed him and wanted him to be there.

'Dad,' she said to him in her mind (she often talked to him in her mind), 'if you were with us here it wouldn't be so bad. It's not fair,' she added. 'Why did he have to be killed? Why *my* Dad?' She felt very angry against God. He was in charge of everything and He had let her Dad be killed. She never told anybody about the feelings she had, she just went away and stood on The Debry and felt bitter. Dad would have taken them to all the exciting places in London, thought Heather, he'd have taken them to the Zoo. Everything would be different she felt if only her father were still alive. Somehow she would have stood up to the kids in school better if Dad were around. Heather hated her school more than anything, and just thinking of it made her clench her fists inside her coat pockets. The children were awful, they had fights all over the place, even the school corridors, and none of the teachers seemed to care. Her own class was the worst in the school, and Heather knew it. They had a nice teacher—she liked him very much really, but he couldn't keep the children in order, so there was always a din going on in her classroom. Children crawled over each other's desks and ran out of the open door and off into the playground or to play hide and seek in the cloakroom whenever they felt like it, and no one took any notice of Mr. Hunt's roaring at them to come back. Nobody learnt anything.

Heather had given up trying. In Cornwall she'd been a leader, scoring lots of points and coming top in tests and things, but what was the good here? She felt savage and angry with her mother for bringing them to London. She forgot all about the things that had made them come—they had to move out of the firm's house within a year, and anyway Mrs. Pendray wanted to get far away from the place where the accident had happened and wanted to be near her parents. Heather forgot that she'd been as keen as anyone to come. She just wanted to go back and have all the nice things she'd lost—her little pink bedroom and her nice happy school, and her Cornish friends. And it was in that sort of mood, standing in The Debry with her fists clenched furiously in her coat pockets and a bitter scowl on her face, that she saw the younger members of the Sterk gang tormenting a cat.

2

AT first she didn't know it was the Sterk gang, and she didn't know it was a cat. The children were a bit younger than her. They were all small, skinny and pale, apart from one or two Jamaican ones who were about the same age but bigger than the others. They were kicking and throwing stones at a little greyish creature which had taken shelter inside a rusty doll's pram without any wheels.

Heather thought the children had found a rat, and, fascinated and yet wrinkling up her nose, she came up closer. (She recognized Dennis Sterk, of course, but didn't connect him with the terrible Ted Sterk gang who were all thirteen or fourteen at least.) When Heather got close to the circle of children she thought she heard a mew. Now she was trying very hard to be on friendly terms with all the kids in her school and Trefoil Street and the area round about. She wanted to be like them. She hated being the stranger and left out, the one who spoke differently, sounded her aitches and rolled her 'r's'. And so she was almost going to take up a stone to throw at the rat (or to look as if she was going to anyway), but when she heard the mew she turned to little Dennis Sterk and said,

'But it's a cat, you know—it mewed.'

'Course it's a cat,' he sneered, 'What d'you fink it was—an elephant?'

Then he made a sudden grab into the hood of the pram and picked out the little creature and threw it with all his might as if it were a ball. It landed on three of its paws, and at once a large sharp-edged stone whammed into its little panting side.

Heather could not really explain what happened next. She found that the boy who had thrown the stone was on the floor and she was holding him by the throat and banging his head up and down on the ground—against a stone. She could have gone banging for ever and she didn't know what had

happened to the cat or the other kids. She didn't know who the boy she was banging was. It wasn't Dennis Sterk but there was blood all over his face, and she was glad.

Then she heard a queer bellowing sound a long way behind her. A stab of fear shot through her fury at something in the sound. She stopped banging and turned her head. Charging across The Debry towards her were three very big boys, urged on by the smaller ones who must have gone off to fetch them. Heather knew them by sight—they were Desmond O'Leary and Ted Sterk, and a great loutish boy called Camlin. In less than two months in Trefoil Street Heather had heard all about the Sterk gang. She left her victim and fled blindly.

Heather was long-legged and skinny, so she ran very fast, even though tin cans kept getting under her feet. She got across The Debry very fast, but it sounded like a hunt behind her. She wasn't a bit sorry about attacking a boy younger than herself or for making his head bleed. She was glad and she exulted in it as she ran. But mixed in with exultation was sheer, blind panic in case she in her turn should be caught by the terrible Sterk and his second-in-command. They were well known for bullying and cruelty and would not worry in the least about hitting a girl or someone younger than themselves.

The hunt was blocking off the way back to Trefoil Street, so Heather instinctively fled towards the hoardings on the main road. It was only when she got nearer that she experienced real panic, the hoardings were very high and completely blocked The Debry from the main road. There seemed to be no way through.

Desperately she turned and began to stumble along beside the fence, going towards the railway line, hoping there would be a space soon, wide enough for her to squeeze through—but there wasn't.

The boys were getting close and she tried to run faster, but her legs were trembling and she only seemed to go slower. It was like one of those terrible nightmares—only she knew she wouldn't wake up. Then a stone hit her on the shoulder, and another on the back of her head, then a shower of stones began. Heather thought, 'If they're so busy picking up stones they can't run so fast,' and she wobbled on. There was a corrugated iron fence between her and the railway line. She had no idea what she could do when she reached it. Things like that were meant to be hard to climb. But she didn't have to try, as it happened. At the same time as a large stone hit her on the arm, she felt a hand grabbing the back of her anorak. She turned to put up a fight and the great Sterk whammed his fist right into her face.

Heather was knocked backwards, slipped on a tin can and fell over. She felt a pain in her hip where she'd banged it, and her lip felt as if it was stuck into her teeth. But her Cornis...

She was on her feet in a secon...

at the big boy with her head...

to butt him in the stomach an...

to defend himself. Heather...

feeling the pain in her hip as...

him from the side instead as...

caught him off balance, of c...

to know the trick (it was o...

her) and he staggered, swea...

Heather was heading towar...

and as the hunt had spread...

sort of circle they were no...

could run fast enough she...

much of a start.

Then she felt a violent cr...

right through her, but esp...

knocked her forward on to...

and saw the brick that Cam...

yellow-faced, glowering bu...

murder in his eyes.

And then she saw and...

clearly. Somebody shoute...

Trefoil Street. Camlin's he...

heard Sterk say:

'That's her brother—co...

Heather thought of Da...

scramble to her feet. The...

boys were all running...

2...

into her teeth. But her Cornish blood was up again. She was on her feet in a second and running straight at the big boy with her head down. She made as if to butt him in the stomach and he put out his arms to defend himself. Heather side-stepped quickly, feeling the pain in her hip as she did so and pushed him from the side instead as she ran past him. She caught him off balance, of course. He didn't seem to know the trick (it was one Norman had taught her) and he staggered, swearing horribly. Oh joy! Heather was heading towards Trefoil Street again, and as the hunt had spread out to corner her in a sort of circle they were now all behind her. If she could run fast enough she was safe, but she hadn't much of a start.

Then she felt a violent crash which seemed to go right through her, but especially her shoulder. It knocked her forward on to her knees. She turned and saw the brick that Camlin had thrown and that yellow-faced, glowering bully running at her with murder in his eyes.

And then she saw and heard everything very clearly. Somebody shouted from the direction of Trefoil Street. Camlin's head jerked round and she heard Sterk say:

'That's her brother—come on—let's get *him*!'

Heather thought of David, and at once began to scramble to her feet. Then she saw that the bigger boys were all running towards, not David but

Norman. And behind Norman came Tony.

Sterk got to them first. He was not the leader of his gang for nothing.

'Out of the way, Forrest!' he bellowed, '—and you won't get hurt!'

Tony wavered for a minute. He'd always kept out of the way. It was the only way to live in Trefoil Street, if you weren't Sterk's type. Tony hated Sterk—but secretly. He liked Norman. And there he was, the silly Cornish fool—didn't he know it'd be three on to one, if Tony kept out of the way, that is? It only took a split second for Tony to think all that. And at the end of it he made up his mind just as quickly. His head was down and he was charging in for the tackle.

And that was why the next thing he saw was a body which crashed down in front of him on to its back, letting out a grunt and a sort of yelp as it did so.

Tony looked up, astonished. Norman was now heading for Camlin. The dreaded Sterk lay at Tony's feet groaning and dazed. So Tony sat on his head. Just as he did so there was a peculiar whistle-cum-yodelling noise, and the rest of the Sterks, big and small, turned tail and fled towards the houses. Ted Sterk made a frantic effort, rolled over, throwing Tony off, got up, and followed his gang. In a few minutes the enemy had disappeared.

Norman turned back towards Tony pulling an

23

astonished face. He'd never even touched Camlin. And Camlin had just turned and run. And all the others too! Surely they weren't such cowards as all that?

'It's the cops,' said Tony. 'See the Sterks' lookout?' He pointed to a small boy who was peeping round the corner of the houses. Then he turned back to Norman.

'Ow'd you knock old Ted Sterk down then?' he asked admiringly.

'Judo trick,' said Norman. 'He came at me with his right arm, see? I turned sideways like this—grabbed his wrist and arm, and tipped him over my hip—like this.' He performed the movement in the air, and added,

'When he lands on his back you can kick him under the ear to knock him out if you like—I thought I'd better not.'

'Stone the crows!' said Tony, admiringly, 'I'll have to practise that.' He turned to Heather who was limping up to them looking rather dismal.

'Knocked you about a bit, didn't they, young Evver? What d'you do to them?'

Heather told him.

'Stone me! Aincher got no sense? You should know better than to hit little Jimmy Sterk! Them Sterks looks after one another, they do.'

'I didn't know he was one of the Sterks,' said Heather crossly. 'But I don't suppose it'd have made any difference if I had. I just lost my temper.'

'You should know better than to hit kids smaller than yourself,' said Norman. What on earth was Heather coming to, he thought, she was getting just like all the other kids round here.

'Well, what would you have done?' Heather turned on him furiously, 'Those little kids are all cowards and bullies themselves. They deserve a taste of their own medicine!'

'All right, all right, Hairpin,' said Norman, using his nick-name for her to try and calm her down and show her that he was fond of her really. She looked such a skinny, miserable little thing.

'Better come home and get cleaned up before Mum comes in.'

They hurried back up to the Pendray's flat. Heather went into the bedroom to examine her injuries, while the boys talked about the fight in the living-room. She had a badly-bruised hip and shoulder, but at least Mum needn't know anything about them. Her leg was scraped where she'd fallen on the tin can, and her hands were scratched. Her lip was swollen and cut on the inside by her teeth when Ted Sterk had hit her in the face. But her teeth were all right, and she thought she could tell her mother quite truthfully that she had been running on The Debry and had fallen over. If Mum knew about the fight she would only worry. And there was nothing Mum could *do*.

Heather went and had a wash and changed her skirt and jumper. Then feeling and looking rather better, although she still ached all over, she went back into the living-room and lowered herself carefully into an old brown armchair that was coming unstuffed.

'Well,' said Norman, 'it seems we're in a right old mess now. Tony says the Sterks'll never forget this.'

'They'll lay in wait for us,' put in David rather excitedly. 'They'll attack us from behind.'

'But that's not fair fighting!' burst out Heather indignantly.

'Fair fighting!' Tony almost choked. 'What d'you fink this is—a boxing tournament or somefink?'

'They just don't fight fair, Hairpin old soul,' said Norman, seeing Heather's eyes beginning to flash at Tony.

'There's only one thing for it—we'll just have to stick together the whole time. There's some safety in numbers, and if we get attacked at least there's a chance one of us can get away and fetch some help.'

'Like I did for Heather,' interrupted David.

Heather stared.

'You can thank your lucky stars young Dave was watching you from the winder up 'ere,' said Tony. 'He saw them chasing you and came and fetched me and Norman.'

'Oh,' said Heather. She looked at David with new respect. She'd always tended to look down on him as a silly little boy.

'Yes, and it was me thought up about that policeman,' said David. 'I pretended I'd seen one in Clover Street and was showing him which way to come, and the Sterks' look-out thought it was real.'

'Cor!' said Tony. 'He's bright, this kid—maybe we'll beat the Sterk gang after all! They ain't got much up top.' He tapped his head.

'That was great, David,' said Norman, looking admiringly too, and David preened himself.

'It's time somebody beat the Sterk gang,' remarked Heather. 'We should have a gang of our own.'

'There's only us four,' said Tony. 'Sterk's got about twelve in his, mostly big-uns.'

'We could get some of the Trefoil Street kids in,' said Heather.

'Well, they're all the ones what Sterk bullies, they wouldn't be no use. They're all the weak ones. All the strong ones are in Sterk's gang,' said Tony.

'We could train them. We could teach them some judo,' said Heather eagerly. 'We could organize them.'

'We don't want to get like Sterk and that lot,' said Norman firmly.

'No, but I mean a good gang,' said Heather. 'Our gang could stick up for all the weak things, all the little kids they frighten, and the animals they hurt. We could put things right around here.'

'Yes,' said David, who was really enthusiastic too, 'the Pendray gang—that's us.'

Norman and Tony looked at each other, and Heather said grandly,

'And have they fixed the where and when, and shall Trelawney die?

Here's twenty thousand Cornishmen will know the reason why.'

Norman grinned. It was his favourite poem and she knew it.

Tony said, 'Cor, blimey! You all right in the head or something?'

Norman couldn't help feeling something must be done, after that.

3

THE 'Pendray gang' did not really begin to do anything for quite some time, however. Several things happened which took their minds off Sterk and his friends.

It began with Mr. Lane, the Vicar from the nearby Church, coming to visit Mum one evening, and inviting her to bring the whole family on an outing he was arranging to the West End to see the Christmas lights. They were all very excited and talked of nothing else for the whole week before.

The 'outing' went up to the West End in a rickety old coach—the property of the church it seemed—driven by a young Jamaican called Des. Des threw the coach round corners, braked suddenly and altogether made the ride as much like a switchback as possible, without the ups and downs. The Vicar had intended to stand in the gangway explaining what part of London they were in, and pointing out places of interest, but he was thrown about all over the place, frequently landing on people's laps. Fortunately for the sitters he was a thin man, quite light and athletic, so no real damage was done to anyone.

When they got to Regent Street the children found they were in the London they'd dreamed about.

There were great shop windows full of exciting things, hundreds of people surging about on the pavements, traffic filling the wide road, and away up in the dark sky hung the 'lights' they had come to see. They were slung across the street, all the way up to Oxford Circus, and each one was the same. The Vicar explained that the theme of the decorations this year was a crown. Right in the centre of the street, up in the air, hung a huge gold and silver crown and thousands of tiny twinkling blue, purple and pink stars seemed to be showering all round it, in the frosty air. A little further on the same thing was repeated and so on, all the way up Regent Street to Oxford Circus. Heather thought it was like fireworks that had been frozen solid in the icy air. David got so excited that he yelped:

'Mum—look! It's the Queen's crown!'

'Gosh!' said Norman, with his head sticking out of the coach window, 'This is more like it.'

A man who was trying to fix up a camera on a tripod to get a picture of the crowns, looked up at the coach and grinned,

'It's quicker by Tube, son,' he said.

Norman didn't know what he meant. He stuck his head inside the coach again.

'That man was an American,' he said to Heather, 'I'm sure he was an American.'

There was a dark-haired girl with a round cheerful face sitting in the seat behind them. She bobbed up and put her nose over the back of the seat:

'I should think about one person in a hundred out there is a real Londoner,' she said.

Heather and Norman could hardly believe this. They both turned back to the window at once to examine the crowd. At first the people just looked like ordinary English people, and the children saw no reason why they shouldn't all be Londoners. Then Heather spotted a group of Indian ladies wearing beautiful saris under their fur coats, and almost at the same time Norman saw a man who couldn't be anything but Chinese. From then on they had a game to see who could spot the most foreigners. The dark-haired girl joined in, and so did a younger one sitting next to her. Heather soon found out that these two were Mr. Lane's daughters. The younger one was Judith, and the dark-haired one was Rachel. She was almost exactly the same age as Heather, and they began to be friends at once.

When they got out of the coach at Trafalgar Square, the *Spot the Foreigner* game became even easier. There were crowds of people strolling about, looking at the great tree, the crib, the fountains, and the huge lions at the foot of Nelson's column. A band was playing Christmas carols, and there were a lot of people crowding around them and singing. Most of the Pendray's coachload joined in the singing, including Mrs. Pendray and David. But Heather and Norman, Rachel and Judith wandered

about among the crowds, listening for people speaking in foreign languages.

By the end of the evening Norman had fifty-two definite foreigners and fifteen possibles. Heather and Rachel, who were doing it between them, and talking about themselves at the same time, only had twenty-three definites and four possibles. Judith had twelve. She wasn't sure whether they were definites or possibles, for she was only seven and had quite a job to pick out foreign languages. In the end she'd abandoned the game and gone back to her father and mother with the carol-singers.

Mrs. Pendray and David enjoyed the singing. The band played *Away in a Manger*, *While Shepherds watched* and *Once in Royal David's City*. David suddenly noticed the words of the last one and began to try and puzzle them out. He couldn't make out what anyone called David had had to do with the Christmas story (which he knew quite well). None of the other carols mentioned him at all, but this carol made David seem quite important. *Royal David's City* . . . London was a city . . . the huge stone lions, and the great gold and silver crowns, the moving wide-awake crowds and the quiet little crib over there behind the band all got confused in David's mind and he began to get London and Bethlehem all mixed up. In fact he began to think that the Lord Jesus had really been born in a place like Trafalgar Square. Which was odd because there weren't any sheep around. In fact, David hadn't seen a single sheep for months. And the Bible didn't say anything about great big lions guarding the crib either . . .

'You getting sleepy, old soul?' said Mum, bending down and smiling. 'Come on—back to the coach now.'

David blinked. Of course he wasn't sleepy—he'd just been having a think. But he was surprised how his feet kept stumbling while they were walking back to the coach . . .

After the 'Outing', all the Pendrays were even more anxious to see all the sights of London, and talked of nothing else, even during the Christmas holiday (which they spent at Streatham).

At last Grandad Parker promised he would take

them all to Madame Tussaud's after Christmas. It was just the thing to cheer you up and stop that flat 'after-Christmas' feeling, he said. There were statues of all the pop stars; there were policemen and keepers standing around so still and so life-like that you couldn't tell which ones were real and which were wax; there was 'The Sleeping Beauty' who seemed to be breathing; and finally the Hall of Mirrors and the Chamber of Horrors. They would have lunch out at Lyons, and if they had time they would go to the Planetarium in the afternoon.

Heather was so excited at the thought of all this that she forgot all about Sterks, and school and how she hated Trefoil Street, and just thought about all the things she would have to tell her Cornish friends when next she saw any of them. Having something to look forward to certainly helped that first day back at Trefoil Street when Mum had gone back to work, and the three children settled down to find something to do till she should come back.

Tony came in and he and Norman got working on the model plane and car kits they'd had for Christmas. David was very anxious to do the same and sat around watching eagerly for any odd jobs that the bigger ones cared to give him. Heather tried to settle down to her new jig-saw puzzle, but she felt tired and rather depressed—wishy-washy in fact. Thank goodness they were going to be out all day tomorrow with Grandad. The battered electric fire, peeling wall-paper and cracked ceilings looked even worse in Mum's absence. She kept longing for a nice cosy coal fire and a furry rug to stretch out on.

It was only when she was undressing for bed at her usual time that she noticed the spots. They were all up her arms and legs. In places they were so thick they'd all run together making blotches. Heather was horrified. Her only thought was that Mum musn't see them. She peered anxiously into the mirror—no, there were none on her face. Quickly she jumped into bed and pulled the clothes up to her neck. In the morning they'll be gone, she thought, or if they aren't Mum'll be so busy getting off to work she won't have time to notice anything. Anyway, she felt better now she was lying down. She felt fine. There couldn't be anything wrong with her. It was good to be in bed.

She was very tired and slept soundly. She awoke in the morning to hear her mother whispering to someone,

'I can't very well go to work, can I?'

There was something rather alarming about her mother's voice. And Heather opened her eyes and turned her head. The first thing she saw was her own arm, which she must have uncovered in her sleep. It was, if anything, spottier than it had been last night. She quickly stuck it under the blanket. The next thing she saw was her grandfather with his overcoat on; then her mother's face looking over his shoulder. They were standing in the doorway. When Grandad Parker saw she was awake, he said with that untruthful sort of joviality that grown-ups put on when there's nothing to laugh about,

'Well, what've you been doing to yourself, eh, young Heather?'

Heather could see by their faces that they were worried about the spots.

'They're nothing,' she said quickly, 'I've had them for ages. They come up and then they just disappear again. I think it's something I've eaten. I feel fine. I'm getting up now.'

She swung her legs over the side of the creaky bed—the side furthest away from the grown-ups in case the spots showed again.

'Come here, dear,' said Mum in her comfortable voice. Heather went over, pulling down the sleeve of her pyjama jacket.

'It's a rash you've had before, is it?' said Mum, looking her straight in the eye.

It was hard to lie to Mum. 'Yes,' said Heather, thinking hard of Madame Tussaud's.

'Mum put her hand on Heather's forehead and felt it. Then she put both her hands on Heather's neck and felt there. Then she looked at Grandad in the way grown-ups have when what they suspect is proved true.

'Glands,' said Mum.

36

'I'll go and get the doctor to confirm it,' said Grandad. 'I'll ring up your office too while I'm in the phone box, and if you want to go to work tomorrow Grandma'll come over and stay with her.'

'What's the matter? I don't want a doctor! There's nothing wrong with me!' cried Heather, in alarm. 'We're going to Madame Tussaud's, we'll be late if we have to wait for the doctor to come first.'

But it was no good protesting. Mum was kind, but firm. As far as Heather was concerned Madame Tussaud's was out. Mum had diagnosed German measles.

When the doctor came he agreed with her, and Madame Tussaud's was ruled out for the boys as well, since German measles is very catching. To help them over their disappointment Grandad Parker stayed with them all day, and promised that they would all go to the waxworks in a week's time when Heather was better.

But this didn't really help. Heather's spots were beginning to fade when Norman's appeared. And his were just going when David got some. So the whole holiday was wasted and miserable. School began again before either of the boys was allowed to go back, and so Heather had to go on her own. She was very babyish and made a scene.

'I had to waste the holidays having German measles,' she raged. 'I ought to be allowed to have a holiday now instead!'

There was quite a fuss. But Mum stuck to her point. She was very sorry about everything, she said, but she couldn't see why Heather wanted to go on staying in the flat all day when she'd done nothing but complain about it for the past ten days. She must go to school and she'd find she'd enjoy it.

Heather left that first morning in a very bad temper indeed. She was only slightly relieved by the sight of Tony waiting about in the street outside.

'Going my way?' he asked nonchalantly, and fell into step beside her. (Norman had asked him to do this because of the Sterks).

Actually it wasn't a bad walk to school at all, only Heather was determined to sulk and be miserable. Tony'd been making lots of plans for the Pendray Gang. He'd been talking about some of them with Norman while Heather had been spotty, and some of them he'd thought up on his own while Norman had been spotty.

'We're going to call it a Watch Committee, not the Pendray Gang. Norm doesn't like having a Gang. What d'you fink?'

'Ugh,' said Heather grudgingly. She thought Watch Committee was a terrific name but she was irritated by the way Tony always called her brother 'Norm'.

Tony went on without noticing:

'We're gonna have judo practices in my flat, cos the people down below are deaf. I got a book on judo out of the library. And we got some new members an' all.' He'd been recruiting for the Watch Committee in Trefoil Street and he'd got a partly-Portuguese girl called Inez, and there was a boy down the end of the street called Conrad who'd join. Inez was in Heather's class at school, and she didn't like her much because she was so uncertain-tempered. Conrad was a very quiet boy, about twelve years old. He lived alone with his dad because his mum had run away.

So now there were six in the Watch Committee.

'I got the tactics worked out an' all,' went on Tony proudly, 'just like a football match——'

'What d'you mean—tactics?' asked Heather.

'What we each got to do when we goes into action against them Sterks. I fink we'll beat 'em 'ands down if we got some plan——oops! There's me bus!'

He rushed off, and Heather dawdled on to school. She arrived late—deliberately. But she'd forgotten that nobody did anything about lateness in this school. She just walked into her class and nobody took any notice. To make up for this, Heather behaved as badly as possible for the rest of the day and succeeded in getting herself kept in after school as a punishment. There were several children being kept in—for rudeness, laziness and disobedience. Mr. Hunt was very near to giving in his resignation that day.

Heather felt resentful at being punished for her crimes, and so made her way home in a worse temper than ever. At the bottom of all this was a fear that she would be punished for her ill-temper by meeting some Sterks in Clover Street just when there was nobody with her to take her side.

But there she was quite wrong. Because half way down the Main Road she bumped into Rachel Lane.

'Oh, good!' said Rachel. 'Just right! I was coming to your house.' Then she went a bit shy and said,

'Do you think you could come to tea on Saturday?'

Heather was astonished and pleased. Just when she knew she didn't deserve it something nice had happened. All the while she was telling Rachel she'd like to very much, and finding out where to go and what time and all that, deep down inside a little voice was saying to her,

'Whatever would Rachel be saying if she could see the way you made a scene with Mum, and then the way you cheeked Mr. Hunt?'

'Crummy!' thought Heather. 'It's a good thing Rachel doesn't know what I'm really like or she'd never have asked me.'

4

THIS idea did not, of course, stop her from going to tea with Rachel. But it did make her try to behave better towards Mum and David and Norman, in the meantime. It was nice to have something to look forward to, something that was specially for her. Rachel said that later on the boys must come to tea, but this time it was to be just Heather.

Mrs. Lane had prepared a very special tea—almost as if it were somebody's birthday, but it wasn't. There were potatoes baked in their jackets, with butter and grated cheese inside them; sausages on sticks; and hard-boiled eggs and salad. After that there were crumpets, toasted by the fire and dripping with butter and there was a choice of honey, or jam, or Marmite to go on them. And finally—to fill in the spaces—there was jelly and ice-cream. And everyone kept urging Heather to have a second helping because she needed to get fatter.

After tea the children helped with the clearing away and washing up, and then retired to the play-room. The Vicarage was quite a large house. Rachel and Judith kept all their things in a big, semi-basement room which looked out on to the back

garden. This play-room smelt strongly of mice, which was because Rachel kept them as pets——

'I'm a sort of mouse-breeder for my whole school,' she said proudly, 'and anyone else who wants them in West Norwood and Dulwich. Do *you* want some?'

Heather did not want to offend her, as they were obviously Rachel's pride and joy. But mice were not her particular favourites.

'I don't know that Mum would let me,' she said truthfully, and began to wander round looking at the cages and asking questions about what you have to do to make mice comfortable and happy and so on. Rachel was only too glad to explain, and Heather, listening to her, got quite interested in mouse breeding. If she took some home in a shoe-box, she thought, the family would have to rally round and help her. Norman could easily make a cage.

'Oh goodness!' she said, at that point, reaching a cage in the corner of the room, 'What's this? Why, you've got a guinea-pig, too!'

'That's Humphrey,' said Rachel proudly. 'Do you like him?' Would you like to have him out?'

Humphrey had gentle sad eyes and long ginger fur, and Heather cuddled down in the big old arm-chair and held him very tenderly on her lap. She felt so envious of Rachel. Rachel had all these animals, and a room of her own, and a father, and she went to a marvellous school where they wore a uniform and it was so large you could stay there right up to the Sixth Form. Trefoil Street might even be bearable if she could have a guinea-pig and go to Rachel's school, thought Heather. Would Mum let her keep a guinea-pig in the bedroom? He wouldn't be nearly as much trouble as a dog or a cat. And much better than mice . . .

Rachel knelt down and began to clean out Humphrey's cage. 'Heather,' she said all at once, 'would you like to come ice-skating with us one day?'

'Ice-skating!' breathed Heather, 'Where? Oh dear—I haven't got any skates.'

'You hire them,' said Rachel, 'at the rink. It's quite near here and maybe your brothers could come too. Daddy comes sometimes with us.

'It would be marvellous,' said Heather, feeling on top of the world again at once, 'I've always wanted to skate. Is it hard?'

'Not very. And at least it's something we've got in London that you haven't got in Cornwall.'

'There are lots of things in London, really,' said Heather, 'if only you can get them.'

As soon as she got home that evening she told the family about skating. And then Mum, without really meaning to, poured cold water over the whole idea.

'Ice-skating's so expensive, dears,' she said. 'You have to go such a lot if you want to do it properly, and that'd cost a fortune.'

The boys looked disappointed, as they had no money left after Christmas. But Heather became furious.

'Everything I want to do gets stopped!' she flared at Mum. And then stamped out of the room and slammed the door as hard as she could. She couldn't care less if the people downstairs complained. In fact, she hoped they would.

She woke up next morning sullen and bitter all over again. Which was a pity, because Mum had suggested that they all go to Mr. Lane's Family Service at church. And Heather would have enjoyed it a lot if she hadn't been in the wrong kind of mood.

The Family Service was a joining-in kind of

service with something for everyone. This was not always intentional. For instance, Tony (who had come with them) spent some of his time sizing up the Curate and deciding whether he'd do better as a full-back or centre-half, and some more time trying to make up a mental football team from among the choirboys and the fathers in the congregation. David enjoyed the Bible-reading most, because it was all about King David and some fierce battles, and was read very loudly by a boy about his own age. Norman enjoyed the Vicar's talk; and Heather tried not to enjoy the singing.

The Vicar didn't preach a sermon, and his talk was hardly even a talk, since he asked a lot of questions to begin with, and the people in the congregation called out answers. Heather hadn't meant to be interested, but quite soon she couldn't help it, for one of the Vicar's questions made all the resentment come bubbling up to the top of her.

'What is your idea,' asked Mr. Lane, 'of the place you'd most hate to have to live in?'

A fair-haired girl near the front, put up her hand and said,

'Prison.'

Heather had a sudden savage longing to bawl out, 'Trefoil Street!'

at the top of her voice. She didn't know, of course, but the Vicar wouldn't have minded if she had. He liked honest answers. He went on to get a lot more people to tell him their ideas of horrible places. Some said they would hate to live anywhere dark and smelly, with rats and mice. The Pendrays all noticed how Rachel's back went stiff with indignation when mice were mentioned—she was sitting up just in front of them, and she began to wriggle and get ready to say something. But then they all had a surprise because a rather hoarse voice came from their own row and said:

'I think it don't really matter how awful the place is, as long as the people's friendly. What's worst is when you ain't got no friends and you're afraid to go out and that.'

It was Tony. Mr. Lane looked pleased that he'd spoken:

'Yes, I'd agree that's the worst of the lot, Tony. Nothing's quite so bad if you've got friends to share it with. But I'll tell you why I asked that question—it's because this is just how the world must have seemed to Jesus, the Son of God, when He came here to live with us. After Heaven, our world would seem like a prison to Him. We think some parts are wonderful. But if we'd been to Heaven and seen what it's like, even our best places would seem dull afterwards,—even ugly!'

'Cornwall?' thought Norman in surprise, 'could anywhere beat Cornwall?' Then he glanced at Tony, who happened to be thinking,

'What about Margate? And what about Brixton

Park? They ain't dull and ugly—how could Heaven be better?'

Heather thought:

'Well, anywhere'd be better than Trefoil Street,' and settled down into her gloom. But the Vicar was going on:

'Jesus wasn't at all afraid of the worst places on earth. He came to a dirty old stable for a start—plenty of rats there, I expect—' (being Rachel's father he left mice out of it) '—overcrowded too—with the animals belonging to all the travellers in Bethlehem. Certainly no one would *want* to be born in a place like that . . . '

Heather actually felt a twinge of shame. Mr. Lane made it sound worse than the flat in Trefoil Street.

'Jesus was God Himself,' he went on, 'the Prince of Heaven. The King of the World. But He wasn't afraid to go anywhere. You look in any of the four Gospels which tell the story of His life, and see if you can find a place where Jesus was afraid. Lots of times His friends were terrified. But not Jesus. The worst time of all was when the people who hated Him marched Him away to put Him to death. All His friends ran away then. But Jesus didn't run away. He fought with death itself—and He won . . . '

When he said that, Norman saw a warrior in shining armour delivering the death blow to a dark, poisonous serpent—cutting its coils from Him, one by one . . .

Tony saw a heroic secret agent firing a ray-gun into the face of a sinister hooded figure . . .

But Heather remembered the real story . . . she saw a dark hillside, and the soldiers diving for cover as the great rocks rolled aside with the noise of thunder, and she saw a young man, strong and unafraid . . .

'And now,' said the Vicar, 'He's alive for ever. He's mightier than any person or anything we have to fight against. And He has promised to be with us if we belong to Him. If you want to be on His side, ask Him. He can hear you, even when you don't speak aloud. And He'll come because this is His promise, "I will never refuse anyone who comes to Me." '

Heather had got really interested by now. But just at that moment David knocked his match-box lorry on to the floor. (He'd been quietly playing with it on the seat, unknown to Mum who wouldn't have let him.) Heather got so confused and cross because David began grovelling on the floor under the seat, and people turned and looked to see what the bang had been, that by the time she had recovered herself it was the closing hymn and so she'd missed whatever else had been said.

But she'd heard enough to remember it later in the week when she was coming home from another evening spent with Rachel and Judith, Humphrey and the mice. It was about eight o'clock, and dark, of course, and as she came down the hill towards the main road Heather got very afraid. She wasn't afraid of the main road, or of crossing it, but she was distinctly nervous at the thought of having to walk half way up Clover Street before she could turn off into Trefoil Street. The Sterk gang all lived in Clover Street. Oh, why hadn't she asked Norman and Tony to come to the Vicarage and meet her? The Sterks often hung around after dark—and they were never up to any good, of course.

She began to walk slower and slower as she neared the main road, and then quite suddenly, because she was hoping for some help, the words the Vicar had said on Sunday came into her mind,

'*He's mightier than anything we have to fight against...*'

And what else?

'*He's promised to be with us if we belong to Him.*' You only have to ask, Mr. Lane had said, and He would take you, because of His promise. You only have to ask, repeated Heather to herself. And at that point she realized that it was much, much more difficult to ask than it had sounded. It was the hardest thing in the world. It wasn't that she didn't believe that He could hear her. In fact, she felt quite sure that He could hear all her thoughts—even when she didn't want Him to. That was what made her so uncomfortable all of a sudden. She felt that she couldn't possibly ask Him to help her because she just didn't deserve it. Jesus was just too good for her, Heather Pendray, bad-tempered and ugly inside.

'*If you want to be on His side, ask Him . . . and He'll come*'. She was nearly at the main road now. She could see the turning into Clover Street on the other side. She stopped quite still, and she could hear shouts and whistles. They were out, then, just as she'd feared.

'I need You,' she said, '*You're* not afraid of Sterks . . . not afraid of anything.' Would He really help her, she wondered, there were so many other things she needed help on too . . . When she thought that it was as if a voice had said to her,

'Now, that's a bit more like it!'
and she remembered that you had to be on *His* side, not just have Him on yours when it suited you. And once she'd thought that, she found she'd made up her mind.

'Oh, please,' she said, 'I *do* want to be on Your side. I'll do my best if You'll help me. Please make me belong to You and be with me from now on.'

She stood there for a minute, feeling ever so relieved. There wasn't anything else she could do and it was all up to Him now. She was feeling better already, and she marched off towards the main road, getting more and more springy at every step. She was glad she was going to Trefoil Street. *He* didn't mind those sort of places, so why should she? There was a lot to be done, and she could hardly wait to begin. She crossed the main road and hurried towards the Clover Street turning. And right on the corner she nearly jumped out of her skin! For someone came charging round and banged right into her. At first she was quite sure it was a Sterk—then she found it was a small boy, and he was crying.

Heather swung round and caught him by the shoulder,

'Whatever's the matter?'

The boy recognized that she was friendly, and turned round rubbing his eyes with his fists.

'They've pinched my cap—and my scarf—the cowards,' he jerked his thumb back up Clover Street, and she saw what she had dreaded—a crowd of Sterks around a street lamp just beyond the Trefoil Street turning.

'I was coming home from Cubs,' said the boy. He was crying with rage as much as anything. 'Eight of 'em on to one—look—they chucked my cap up on the wall—I'll get into trouble with my mum—they're new——'

'Look—wait here on the corner,' said Heather, 'I'll get my brother and his friends. We'll get your things back, don't worry.'

She felt excited, but rather nervous. This was exactly the sort of thing the Watch Committee had been practising for for weeks. Tony had explained the tactics. All Heather had to do now was get to Inez' doorstep and whistle the signal. Then out would rush the members of the

She began to move stealthily

of her dark raincoat and the sha

Ahead of her she could pick out

Sterk. Then there were a coup

Tommy O'Leary and a Wes

didn't know the others. Most

backs to her, or their heads turn

watching two more small

Clover Street. Heather got q

slipped round the corner and

Then, not caring any more wh

since now they couldn't block

broke into a run, as fast as she

doorstep.

course, and as she came down the hill towards
the main road Heather got very afraid. She wasn't
afraid of the main road, or of crossing it, but she
was distinctly nervous at the thought of having to
walk half way up Clover Street before she could
turn off into Trefoil Street. The Sterk gang all lived
in Clover Street. Oh, why hadn't she asked Norman
and Tony to come to the Vicarage and meet her?
The Sterks often hung around after dark—and they
were never up to any good, of course.

She began to walk slower and slower as she neared
the main road, and then quite suddenly, because she
was hoping for some help, the words the Vicar had
said on Sunday came into her mind,

*'He's mightier than anything we have to fight
against...'*
And what else?

'He's promised to be with us if we belong to Him.'
You only have to ask, Mr. Lane had said, and He
would take you, because of His promise. You only
have to ask, repeated Heather to herself. And at that
point she realized that it was much, much more
difficult to ask than it had sounded. It was the
hardest thing in the world. It wasn't that she didn't
believe that He could hear her. In fact, she felt quite
sure that He could hear all her thoughts—even when
she didn't want Him to. That was what made her so
uncomfortable all of a sudden. She felt that she
couldn't possibly ask Him to help her because she

just didn't deserve it. Jesus was just too good ... her, Heather Pendray, bad-tempered and ugly inside.

'*If you want to be on His side, ask Him . . . and He'll come*'. She was nearly at the main road now. She could see the turning into Clover Street on the other side. She stopped quite still, and she could hear shouts and whistles. They were out, then, just as she'd feared.

'I need You,' she said, '*You're* not afraid of Sterks . . . not afraid of anything.' Would He really help her, she wondered, there were so many other things she needed help on too . . . When she thought that it was as if a voice had said to her,

'Now, that's a bit more like it!'

and she remembered that you had to be on *His* side, not just have Him on yours when it suited you. And once she'd thought that, she found she'd made up her mind.

'Oh, please,' she said, 'I *do* want to be on Your side. I'll do my best if You'll help me. Please make me belong to You and be with me from now on.'

She stood there for a minute, feeling ever so relieved. There wasn't anything else she could do and it was all up to Him now. She was feeling better already, and she marched off towards the main road, getting more and more springy at every step. She was glad she was going to Trefoil Street. *He* didn't mind those sort of places, so why should she? There was a lot to be done, and she could hardly wait to begin. She crossed the main road and hurried towards the Clover Street turning. And right on the corner she nearly jumped out of her skin! For someone came charging round and banged right into her. At first she was quite sure it was a Sterk—then she found it was a small boy, and he was crying.

Heather swung round and caught him by the shoulder,

'Whatever's the matter?'

The boy recognized that she was friendly, and turned round rubbing his eyes with his fists.

'They've pinched my cap—and my scarf—the cowards,' he jerked his thumb back up Clover Street, and she saw what she had dreaded—a crowd of Sterks around a street lamp just beyond the Trefoil Street turning.

'I was coming home from Cubs,' said the boy. He was crying with rage as much as anything. 'Eight of 'em on to one—look—they chucked my cap up on the wall—I'll get into trouble with my mum—they're new——'

'Look—wait here on the corner,' said Heather, 'I'll get my brother and his friends. We'll get your things back, don't worry.'

She felt excited, but rather nervous. This was exactly the sort of thing the Watch Committee had been practising for for weeks. Tony had explained the tactics. All Heather had to do now was get to Inez' doorstep and whistle the signal. Then out would rush the members of the Watch Committee.

She began to move stealthily up the road, glad of her dark raincoat and the shadows of the houses. Ahead of her she could pick out Jimmy and Dennis Sterk. Then there were a couple of bigger ones— Tommy O'Leary and a West Indian boy. She didn't know the others. Most of them had their backs to her, or their heads turned away. They were watching two more small boys coming down Clover Street. Heather got quite close to them, slipped round the corner and into Trefoil Street. Then, not caring any more whether they heard her, since now they couldn't block her way home, she broke into a run, as fast as she could towards Inez' doorstep.

5

WHETHER it was because she was panting, or because her mouth was dry, or her fingers were shaking with excitement, Heather couldn't get the whistle to come. She stuck her two fingers in her mouth, rolled her tongue up the way Tony had shown her, and blew hard—but all she could get was a bit of a squeak. Bother! She blew and blew, nearly crying with frustration. Then the door of the house opened and out popped Inez.

'I was looking through the window,' she said, coolly. 'You trying to do the whistle?' She went on, 'Here! Look!' She stuck two fingers in her mouth and blew. A beautiful clear, long high-pitched sound came out. Two shorts and a long.

The boys in Clover Street were whooping and yelling round the two petrified boys who were also Cubs. But they heard the whistle in spite of their noise, and paused for a moment, recognizing it as a signal, but not quite sure what it meant. Then, since there were no signs of danger, they went on enjoying themselves, throwing the little boys' caps to each other and trying to land them on the wall, as they'd done the other one. Some of them caught hold of the victims and pulled their scarves off, too.

They hit one so that he went sprawling.

'Oh, come on, Norman!' Heather was hopping up and down in the doorway. 'We'll have to get those scarves off them, Inez. I don't know how we can reach the caps. Anyway, I'll go for Jimmy Sterk and you get that O'Leary kid. They've got the scarves in their hands. Oh, come on, Norman!'

Right then there was a slam of a front door and another slam quite close to it, then several sets of running footsteps.

'This way,' yelled Heather, and she and Inez pelted out of the doorway and led the attack on the surprised Sterks. Conrad came running out of his house as they passed, and joined in. Behind them she could hear Norman, Tony and David. They all pounded towards the astonished Sterks.

What happened next astonished the Watch Committee just as much. The enemy just turned and fled. One minute there were eight Sterks having a whale of a time round a lamp post and two victims, the next there was nobody. Even the victims had run for dear life!

'My life!' said Tony, disappointedly. 'Thought we was going to have some action.'

Inez shrugged her shoulders and pulled a face.

'Dunno what we all came out for!'

'Well, it worked all right, didn't it?' said Norman. 'Come on, Tony, do your stuff and make a back for me to get those caps down. For all we know they're running to fetch their big brothers. Keep a look-out, you others.'

Tony obligingly bent his back and Norman climbed up high enough to unhook the two caps that had been landed on the wall. David found the third one and a scarf in the gutter. Heather found another scarf on the pavement.

'They must have run off with the other one,' said Conrad.

They searched around but couldn't find the third one. Then they all marched down the road and gave their spoils of war back to the rightful owners. The three Cubs were very pleased and surprised. They had stayed at the corner by the main road watching to see what would happen.

'From now on, Tony told them, 'we'll have someone on the watch on your Cub night, so don't be scared of them. If they do anything you just run to number 18, Trefoil Street, see, and knock on her door'—he pointed to Inez. 'She'll call us, see, so don't you worry and you can tell all your friends, too. We got a Watch Committee going on here.'

The boys nodded, looking admiringly at the Watch Committee, and then charged off home. They hadn't even lost the scarf because one of them had picked his up as he'd run away.

There was still no sign of Sterks as the Watch Committee went back up the street.

'Can't understand it,' said Tony, 'You wouldn't think they were such cowards as that. After all, there's more of them than us.'

'I bet they're so surprised at anyone standing up to them they don't know what to do,' said Norman. 'They'll think of something one day, though. We'd better be on our guard. I don't think we can put them down as easily as all that.'

Heather felt sure that they'd been helped. She tried to tell Norman a bit about it, when they were on their own, and was encouraged to find that he, too, believed it.

'If we belong to Him, it means we're fighting on His side,' said Norman. 'It stands to reason He's going to help us. But that doesn't mean it's always going to be as easy as this.'

Just the same, the next few weeks passed very

pleasantly for the Pendrays. Half-term came, and with it an invitation from Rachel to go to the Science Museum one day, and skating another. Grandad Parker came over and gave each of them five shillings to help out their pocket money. Nobody became ill. In fact, nothing happened to spoil any of it. The Science Museum was wonderful, with its experiments which had buttons to press to make things happen, and a floor full of aeroplanes, and another one full of old-fashioned steam-engines. And the skating rink was just as exciting in a different way. The Pendrays had all done some roller-skating, so they got on quite well on the ice—though their ankles were stiff afterwards!

'It's like flying,' said Heather to Rachel as they went round and round, 'it's so smooth and quiet and fast.'

Mr. Lane, who'd come too (but without his back-to-front collar, because he said he fell over less without it) bought them all milk shakes and they sat round a table and watched the skaters glide past.

'London's not so bad, is it?' said Norman, grinning at Heather, and she smiled back feeling quite contented.

She could see now how silly she'd been to fly off the handle just because Mum had said skating was too expensive. If she had just waited quietly, it would have all worked out. Looking back, she couldn't see what she had got into such a temper about, and gave herself a pep talk:

'You do things first and think about them afterwards, my dear,' she said to herself in a superior way. 'Try to pull yourself together.'

She went back to school for the second half of term, determined to work hard. And she was surprised how well she succeeded. She sat by a Jamaican boy called LeRoy Wilson, who thought rulers and pencils were for trying to make rhythm and jazz-band imitations, and that Mr. Hunt was there to be sneered at. On the morning of the first day back, Mr. Hunt was trying to teach some history, and LeRoy was, of course, drumming his 'instruments' on the desk. Heather got mad:

'Shut up, can't you? I want to listen.'

LeRoy was so surprised that he did stop. But he sneered,

'Teacher's pet!'

'So what?' snapped Heather. 'I'm sick and tired of this class—and you especially! I'm bored stiff with doing nothing all day. I'm going to work.'

And so she did—in fact, she wondered why she'd ever stopped, because she'd always enjoyed lessons. Mr. Hunt had got some very interesting things for his class to do, and when he saw that Heather was really trying, he gave her lots of encouragement. Then when LeRoy, and Inez who sat behind her, saw how interested she was, they began to get interested too, and wanted to do the same things.

It spread through the class. Heather found with surprise that the children only wanted a leader and they would behave themselves. Up till now the bad children had been leaders and so the whole class had been bad. Now the cleverer ones began to compete with Heather, and so the class began to work and was quieter, and Mr. Hunt was able to give more time to the slower children.

The Watchers continued to guard the smaller children of Trefoil and Clover Streets from the activities of the Sterks. Now that the evenings were getting lighter, children began to play out in the streets, and the Watch Committee had some rescues to do. Once it was a boy, walking alone down Clover Street, who was attacked by Sterks for no reason except that he was alone and they thought nobody was watching. Another time it was several little children whose ball was taken. Another time it was a cat being tortured. Each time, when the Watch Committee attacked, the Sterks ran away and abandoned their victims. The bigger Sterks kept well out of the way—it was rumoured that Camlin was on probation for helping with a burglary, and that O'Leary had been sent to an Approved School. Ted Sterk was still to be seen around, but he usually contented himself with stone-throwing from a safe distance. The Sterks were clearly afraid of a real fight.

It was getting warmer, as well as lighter. March

was bringing spring-time, but the children didn't notice it at first. Then one day when they went to church there were white, yellow and mauve dots all over the grass.

'Crocuses,' said Heather, 'I'd forgotten about spring.' She stared at the brave little flowers, and then, for the first time for about two months, felt something move inside which hurt. 'Cornwall!' it said.

After that, she saw daffodils and tulips appearing on the flower stalls on the main road, and a week or two later the yellow buds appeared in the garden in front of the church, nodding in the breeze. And the thing inside Heather moved and hurt again, because they'd had a garden full of daffodils in St. Austell. There was never even a window-box in Trefoil Street, and only a few weak-looking weeds on The Debry.

Norman was not so fond of flowers, but he remembered another thing, one day when they were leaning over the railway bridge, looking down towards the station.

'I say, Heather,' he said, 'do you remember the station at St. Austell with the palm-trees on the platform? Tony doesn't believe me that there were any.'

'Oh, there were! There were!' cried Heather, and the picture of the clean, sleepy platform rose up in her mind. 'You ought to come and see, Tony!

There are flower-beds and palm trees all along the platform. Not like these dirty old London stations.'

'Oh, well,' said Tony, shrugging his shoulders cheerfully, 'we got the best football teams, anyway.'

But from then on, Heather was discontented.

'Mum,' she said, as soon as she could, 'Can we go back to Cornwall for the Easter holidays?'

'Oh, no, dear, I'm sorry,' said Mum, 'I really can't afford the fares. Besides, I only have two days off, you see.'

'Can't Norman and David and I go on our own?'

'Oh, no, dear—it's too far. I'll save up and we'll all go in the summer holidays.'

But the summer holidays were such a dreary way off, and the cherry trees blossoming in the park in the last week of term made the thought of the coming holiday having to be spent in a town unbearable.

And then, on the day when the primroses began to appear on the flower-stalls, and Heather was feeling miserable because there was nowhere she could go and see them growing wild, and pick great bunches and tie them up with string—well, on that day she heard that the Lanes were going to spend most of their Easter holiday in Pembrokeshire with Mrs. Lane's sister.

Heather went to tea with Rachel and said goodbye for the next three weeks, and then she walked home gloomily by herself wishing that there was no such thing as a holiday. She would even rather be in school than this, she thought. She slouched along to the top of Clover Street with her head bent.

Then there was a shout and a sound of barking and, looking up, startled, she saw a great black mongrel dog rushing towards her, barking furiously, and behind it, whooping it on, the Sterks large and small, set for the hunt.

6

HEATHER turned and fled. The moment she began running she remembered she should have stood quite still, but how could she stand still when all those Sterks were coming too? And it was certainly the sort of dog that would bite you anyway.

The houses at that end of Clover Street had railings in front of them and steps leading down to the basements. Heather had only gone a few steps when she saw a gate in the railings, partly open, and instinctively knowing that she must put a barrier of some sort between herself and that snarling black creature, she whipped through the gate and slammed it shut. Then she leapt down the steps and, without bothering about whose house it was, opened the side door which led through to the back-yard, ran through that and slammed it shut. There was a bolt, so she bolted it. Then she stood panting and wobbling all over, and listened to the Sterks' voices. Goodness! They'd let the dog into the area! It was barking frantically and snuffling round the door, and they were urging it on from the street.

'It's a stupid, savage dog,' thought Heather, 'just the sort of dog kids like the Sterks *would* get hold of! Thank goodness for that door and the bolt.'

It occurred to her that there might be a way out at the back of the house, so she went on down the narrow dark passage towards the back-yard. It was a rather smelly place and Heather didn't like it much. She wondered who the owners were and hoped she wouldn't meet any of them.

But she did. The back door of the house opened just as she came around the side of the house, and there stood the most weird-looking old man. He was dressed in an assortment of very old clothes, he had a pouchy, lined face, a drooping yellow moustache and hardly any hair. He was thin and stooped. Heather hoped that he was kind. She couldn't see his eyes because of the old tweed cap he wore pulled down over his forehead, but he seemed to be staring at her, as if demanding some explanation.

'Please, sir,' stammered Heather, 'there's a dog—it was chasing me, and——'

The old man let out a roar, a terrifying roar—he was roaring at *her*! It was as if he hadn't heard a word she'd said. Heather turned and ran again. The old man came after her, shaking his fist.

When Heather got to the door, she didn't know which to face, the roaring old man or the savage dog. Then, as she hesitated, feeling nothing could be worse than the dog, the old man let out another crazy bellow, which frightened her out of her wits.

'He's mad!' she thought, fumbling with the bolt. 'Oh, please let that dog be gone away——'

She got the door open, and charged through, avoiding the madman's fist by an inch, and she nearly sobbed with relief when she saw that the Sterks appeared to know the roar and to have run off and their mad dog with them.

The madman didn't come through the door, but she heard him bolt it so she couldn't go back through it. If that dog came back she had no escape. Very cautiously she crept up the steps and poked her nose out, past the railings, the dog had gone a bit further down towards the Trefoil Street end of Clover Street and was sniffing at the bottom of a wall. It had its back to her. The Sterks were sitting on the railings in front of one of their houses. Heather popped back into the area at once.

Would it be any use whistling? One of the Watch Committee might be around—somebody should be on patrol. But if she whistled that would just show the Sterks that she was still here, and now the door was bolted behind her, the Sterks and that dog would get at her before the Watch Committee came on the scene. And how could you use judo on a savage dog? No, she must get out of the area somehow, and try another house. Or else, somehow, get back up Clover Street and find another way round to Trefoil Street. There was no way to get on to The Debry, she knew. But there might be some way around behind the condemned houses on the opposite side of Trefoil Street. If she could just get out of Clover Street . . .

Heather must have waited there about ten minutes. It felt like an hour. She dreaded the return of her enemies, and was scared to poke her nose out into the street again in case this time they were watching. She had never been more wretched in her life, nor felt so alone, and during that ten minutes she despaired and made up her mind.

She would go back to Cornwall. Nothing would make her stay in London any longer. Nobody would keep her. It was no good fighting creatures like the Sterks. You couldn't fight them fairly. They would always win in the end because they didn't care

about how they fought. They're evil, she thought, and they don't care how low they stoop, so how can we beat them without getting evil too? She would go to Cornwall. She would go and live with Grandad and Nanna Pendray. Once she'd got there, Mum would see it was the best thing, and wouldn't try to bring her back. She'd ask Norman to come too, then it wouldn't be so much bother for Mum having to look after them, she argued. All this she thought in ten minutes, shaking and anxious in the smelly area.

It seemed like hours to her, and her desperate decision had made her brave again. She felt she could face anything, even that dog, if she knew that it was the last time and that after that she'd be in Cornwall and wouldn't have to face anything again.

Slowly she crept up the area steps and poked her nose out again. The Sterks had disappeared and their dog was trotting away down the street. As she watched, it turned up Trefoil Street. Heather stood up, stepped on to the pavement, turned her back on the dog and went as quickly and softly as she could back up to the top of Clover Street. She was further away from Trefoil Street, but at least she wasn't trapped any more, and no one had seen her.

It took her a very long time to work her way around to Trefoil Street by way of the derelict houses. They were mostly joined together in terraces, and she had to go right round two more sides of a square before she found a passage with a wall at the end that looked as if she could climb it. She almost turned back and risked Clover Street, but the memory of the fright she'd had was just too much for her.

In the end she did get through to Trefoil Street, though she looked very much the worse for wear. She finally emerged through one of the boarded-up windows—the board had been wrenched loose and not put back properly, so Heather was able to move it and wriggle through the space. She raced across the road and up into the flat. She had never been more pleased with the sight of that shabby old front door in her life.

Norman opened the door to her.

'Where on earth have *you* been? I was just going to come and look for you—what on *earth* have you been doing?'

'Where's Mum?' Heather just wanted to pour it all out to her mother. She was pale and trembling still.

'She's gone in next door to watch telly, with David,' said Norman. 'I needed to work on my Mustang so I stayed here, with Tony. What's happened?'

Heather went into the living room, where the floor was littered with bits of model aeroplanes, instructions for making and pots of special paint.

Tony was sitting in the midst, his face red from bending over a wing right in front of the electric fire.

'Wotcher!' he said, then—'Stone the crows! Where've *you* been?'

Heather sat down and put her face in her hands.

'The Sterks have got a dog now. It's a terrible thing—they set it on to me . . . '

'Why didn't you do the whistle—call the Watch Committee?'

'I couldn't, they know the whistle now, they'd have known where I was—anyway I'm no good at whistling.'

She laid her face down on her shaking arms.

'I'm going to Cornwall.'

'Don't be silly,' said Norman. 'You'll feel better in the morning.'

'Just because of a silly old dog!' said Tony. 'You wouldn't be so daft.'

But Norman knew about Heather's fear of dogs, so he just sat looking worried. There was always so much to worry about in London. He was the 'man of the family' now, and he felt responsible for everything. Underneath his common sense, a longing for Cornwall was stirring in him too.

'I've planned it all,' said Heather, her face still lying on her arms, and turned towards the fire. 'We can live with Grandad and Nanna Pendray in St. Austell and go to our old schools again.'

Norman said nothing. The thought of going back to his old school swelled up inside him.

'What d'you want to do that for?' asked Tony, searching around for the upper and lower halves of the right wing. Tony didn't understand, thought Norman, handing him the cement; he'd never been out of London. He didn't know what it was like. They could go to the sea and swim—the summer term—oh, it was like heaven to think of it, the palm trees on St. Austell Station, the old quiet houses, the flowers in front gardens, the friendly, sunburnt people . . .

'There's no reason why we should live here,' said Heather, 'if we all hate it so. It'd be much less trouble for Mum if she didn't have us to look after— she could give up this flat and go and live with Grandad Parker, and then come and see us in the holidays, or we could go there for holidays. It'd be like being in boarding school, only nicer, because we'd have Grandad and Nanna Pendray to live with.'

'But I don't think Mum would agree,' said Norman, half-persuaded.

'We wouldn't tell her till we'd got there.'

'You mean—you'd run away?' said Tony, his blue eyes goggling.

'We couldn't do that! That's flat!' said Norman, 'Mum'd be worried stiff.'

'No, she wouldn't,' said Heather, sitting up

straight, her cheeks flushed, her eyes bright. 'All we've got to do is ask if we can all spend a few days at Grandad Parker's and then when we've got to Cornwall, we'll write, and then it'll be done and there'll be nothing to worry about.'

'You've forgot something,' said Tony, ' 'ow you going to get there?'

'Walk,' said Heather, 'thumb lifts, perhaps we might get one lift all the way down there—anyway it can't be very far—people walk everywhere, don't they? What about those people who walked from Land's End to John o' Groats?'

'But they were grown-ups, I never heard of children doing it,' objected Norman.

Tony, however, took a different view.

'Well, it ain't as far as John o' Groats, 'cos that's in Scotland. Got an atlas?'

Norman found a thin, rather battered atlas which had lost its cover and they examined the map of Britain which took up pages 6 and 7. It was a political map and just gave the counties and towns, not what the country was like. It didn't look too far to Cornwall, as Tony'd said, nothing like as far as John o' Groats. There was London, a great grey splodge, as big as a county, as big as Rutland, anyhow. And there was Cornwall, coloured pale green. Presumably the colours were accidental, but to Norman and Heather, poring over the pages, they were significant—London grey and ugly, Cornwall

71

green and pleasant.

Norman found himself working out the route—
'Kingston, Weybridge, Woking, Basingstoke, Andover, Salisbury, Yeovil, Exeter, Tavistock, St.
Austell—that's roughly the road anyway. 'Course
we could cut across country sometimes if we were
walking . . . '

'No good going through Kingston,' said Tony,
with the air of one who knew London. 'Take you
hours to get out of London that way. You got to
go to Croydon first. That's not far from here. I
know the way, you go to Crystal Palace, you'd be
out of London then, see, and you could make
straight over to Woking.'

That looked all right on the atlas.

'How long do you think it'd take?' asked Norman.

'A couple of days,' said Heather. 'We'd have to
sleep out, of course.' She felt she could brave anything except the Sterks' dog. Besides, the very
thought of the journey was exciting. One long
marvellous country walk, with picnics all the way,
sleeping under haystacks.

'You've got your sleeping bag,' she said to
Norman. He'd had it new for Crusader camp last
year. It was his birthday present and was very light,
made of terylene, it rolled up very small and was
easy to carry. He'd been using it as an eiderdown
on his bed all this winter, and he was longing to
try it out properly again.

72

'I got a sleeping bag,' said Tony. 'Coo, I think I'll come with you, if you'll wait till the football's over.'

'When's that?' asked Norman, feeling even more encouraged at the thought of someone else to share the responsibility.

'Next Saturday,' said Tony, 'last match.'

'I'm not waiting till then,' said Heather, in dismay, 'I'm going on my own tomorrow.'

The boys persuaded her that this was silly. They would need a few days to make plans, collect some food and see what money they could raise. Anyway, the next day was Tuesday, and Mum still had a holiday from her office. There was a bit of a debate over whether they should take David. In the end they decided that they couldn't leave him to face the Sterks on his own, so if he wanted to come he must be allowed to. He was a tough little boy, and a good walker too.

David did, of course, want to come. He was quite prepared to stay in London and fight the Sterks— even their dog—for all he was worth, but if the others were having an adventure like walking to Cornwall, he wasn't going to be left behind, not David.

So that was that.

Norman had the rest of the week to prove to himself that the Sterks' new dog was a raving maniac and that it would be better to keep out of its way rather than be bitten and get rabies. It was a bit difficult to keep out of its way as you had to go down Clover Street to get anywhere at all from Trefoil Street. Heather was too terrified to venture out of doors, unless accompanied by all three boys. So, bit by bit, the plans for the expedition were made.

Tony made all the difference to Norman's going through with it. He knew the way to Croydon. He had a sleeping bag like Norman's and also plenty of money. He got 10/- a week pocket money and had saved £2 towards a record player, which was his next major ambition. He also asked for an advance on his pocket money over the Easter holidays and turned up on Sunday evening with £3. To Norman it seemed like a fortune. If they didn't spend all of it on food, they might even be able to take a bus when the younger ones were tired. He wasn't sure that they should accept all this from Tony. The Pendrays had only 10/- between them. There was Norman's 4/- pocket money for the whole Easter holiday, Heather's 3/- and David's 2/-; the odd shilling was what they had left over between them from the time before. They only had all this because they'd been thinking of going to the skating rink again. Tony insisted that his £3 must be put in the 'pool'.

'It's like a holiday for me,' he said, 'They'll make me go home again after, but my dad'll send the fare, so I'll be all right.'

7

THEY set off about quarter past eight the following Monday morning. Mum had left for work about a quarter of an hour before. She had made four Cornish pasties on Sunday night, so they could have lunch with Tony or take a picnic out if they wanted to. She was expecting them to spend the next three nights at Grandad Parker's. There was also fruit cake and oranges, and a boiled ham and some butter which she was sending to Grandma Parker to help out with food. Heather felt that it wasn't stealing if they took that with them, since Grandma Parker wouldn't be required to feed them. Unknown to Mum, Norman had sent a post-card to Grandma Parker saying the children were not coming after all.

Tony turned up with a large parcel of food which his mum had sent. She was under the impression that he was going on the camp Mr. Lane's curate was organizing for some of the Youth Club boys, and indeed he had been, except that he'd been down to Kent before, and so preferred the thought of Cornwall—this magical place the Pendrays kept on and on talking about, where it was always sunny and happy and full of games and enjoyment.

Heather had a large polythene bag which Norman had almost forbidden her to bring, because of the danger. Tony had found it. His mum had just had a new cooker, and this polythene bag was around it, and wouldn't it be useful as a ground sheet?

'As long as no one fools about and gets inside it, all right then,' said Norman. '*Only* as a ground sheet, mind.' Heather also had a pair of scissors.

It was the perfect day for setting out on such a journey. The sky was pale blue, and a misty brightness hung about in the air. The sun couldn't be seen properly yet, but when they got on top of the hill they'd see it. They each had two pairs of socks on, their stoutest walking shoes, jeans and their thickest sweaters, under anoraks as well as scarves. Norman insisted that they'd need all these clothes on at night, and it was easier to wear than carry them.

It was uphill going to Upper Norwood, and it was a long way. By the time they'd been walking half an hour they all felt extremely hot and rather thirsty.

'We're nearly there,' said Tony, 'and it's more downhill to Croydon.'

They were all quite determined not to grumble or moan so they plodded on, getting hotter and redder. Because she was so hot and so excited, Heather suffered from a kind of mirage. She was so homesick for a sight of the sea, and so thirsty, she began to imagine that when they got to the top of the hill she would see it, stretched out and shimmering, far away. There were gardens to the houses on the hill and many of them had apple and cherry trees blossoming. Birds were chirping away, and it was not at all like Trefoil Street. She was glad they were going out of London. Everything was merry and happy. It was going to be a glorious adventure, and just there—when they got up to that clear bit at the top of the hill, she would be able to see the sea. There was a warm wind blowing, and the pale pink blossoms nodded against the bright sky. Heather seemed to smell the sea.

They reached the crest of the hill at last, and she got ready to clap her hands and jump with excitement, but—oh dear! Stretched out below was nothing but a world of grey houses. Houses and houses and houses—right up to the very horizon. She could hardly even spot a single tree. Surely the sea wasn't as far away as all that!

'Come on, 'Evver,' shouted Tony. 'Quick march to Croydon.'

Heather pulled herself together, and hurried after the boys. How silly! They hadn't been going any time yet.

By midday they were still trudging along streets with pavements and houses, and had not seen one green field. They'd been sure they'd be in the country in no time! They stopped in a small recreation ground and ate their lunch. They were

77

ravenously hungry and terribly hot. They ate the pasties and most of the cake and finished up with rather a lot of fruit. Tony saw a kiosk and went and bought four 'cokes'. That helped a lot. He also bought four more, because they would be in the heart of the country by tea-time.

Having some of the food inside them didn't make walking easier, for now they were so hot they had to take off their anoraks and carry them. They each took off one pair of socks too, and put them in the anorak pockets.

'We'll have half an hour's rest,' said Norman, 'then we'll get going again. We're bound to get out of the built-up area soon.'

He lay down on his stomach on the grass and began to pore over the atlas. They were in Croydon, and they'd turned right towards Ewell. That wasn't marked on the map, but they were bound to be going in the right direction if they kept going west.

'That only means keeping the sun in your eyes,' thought Norman. 'Darn it! We should've brought sunglasses.'

'Norman!' Heather had crept up beside him; she had her scissors in her hand. 'If you're not too busy would you mind cutting my hair?' she said politely.

'Cutting your hair?' Norman thought she'd gone potty. What on earth did she want to get her hair cut for *now*?

'Yes, very short. I think I'd look like a boy then.

It'd be better if they think we're four boys, won't it?'

Norman hesitated. Heather's hair was shoulder-length. He'd never cut any hair in his life before.

'Yes, go on, it's a good idea,' said Tony. 'Go on! *I'll* do it if you like.'

He picked up a piece of hair and snipped. Did it again and again. Norman watched in admiration.

'Gosh! I do believe you'll be one of those Mayfair hairdressers when you grow up, old soul!'

'Not me! I'm gonna be a footballer. But there's nothing to it really. You just cuts it off, like this.'

When he'd finished, Heather did very well as a boy. Tony'd got it crooked to begin with, so he'd had to cut it shorter one side—then he'd had to cut the other side shorter to match. The result was a real crop.

'What shall we do wiv all this?' said Tony, picking up the handfuls of straight brown hair.

'There's a bin over there,' said David.

They stuffed it in, rather guiltily, and set off again.

'We must try and get to Basingstoke tonight,' said Norman, as they tramped along. 'We'll be about a third of the way then, so if we can keep that up we'll only take three days to be in St. Austell.'

'How far's Basingstoke?' asked David.

'Well, rather a long way,' admitted Norman, 'I think we'll have to try and get a lift.'

There didn't seem much hope of that as long as

79

they were in a built-up area, so they tramped on in silence. They reached Ewell about tea-time, and it was pretty clear that David and Heather had had enough. They were going more and more slowly, their lips pressed tight together so as not to be heard complaining.

'We'll stop and have tea, and then we'll start thumbing,' said Norman. They sat down gratefully on the grass verge of the road—watching the evening traffic thundering by. They ate all Tony's egg sandwiches and an orange each, and drank Tony's cokes. They could have eaten more but Heather said they should keep something for supper. It was amazing how much food four children could get through in a day, thought Norman, and still be hungry.

'Quarter of an hour, sitting here,' he said, 'and we'll thumb too—but it probably won't be much use, they won't want to get out of the stream of traffic to stop.'

He was right. After a quarter of an hour they got up and trudged on, but no one stopped. Norman began to get worried. It was 6.30. Heather said her feet were sore. David said he thought he could do about three more miles—he was determined to keep up with the bigger ones.

'You two sit down,' said Tony. 'Rest your feet. Norman and I'll stand and keep thumbing.'

Heather and David flopped down on the grass

verge, leaning against each other back to back. They were too tired to talk. After about five minutes of frantic thumbing, a Land Rover drew up with a squeal of brakes further down the road. Norman forgot his tiredness and raced up to it.

'Come on,' said Tony to David and Heather. Then he looked at David and saw that his head had dropped forward and he was fast asleep. Heather jumped up, so that poor David woke up with a jerk. 'Go on! Run, 'Evver,' said Tony, 'mustn't keep him waiting, I'll help David.'

Norman was talking to the driver.

'We want to go to Basingstoke,' he said.

'Staines—by-pass,' said the man, 'It's all I can do. I'm going to Windsor.'

Norman knew that Staines was a bit far north of their intended route, so he hesitated.

'Take it or leave it,' said the man, 'I can drop you on the A30 to Basingstoke.'

Heather had come puffing up, and behind them Tony was running with David.

'Thanks,' said Norman, making his decision quickly, 'it's very kind of you, it'll do nicely.'

He helped Heather into the back, then David, then he and Tony squeezed in after them. The Land Rover started up.

'D'you live in Basingstoke?' said the driver.

'Yes,' said Tony, quickly. Norman felt panic-stricken. They hadn't thought of a story to tell if they were asked questions.

'What you doing all this way away then?' said the man. 'Long way from home, aren't you?'

'We came up to Crystal Palace, see,' said Tony, 'on an excursion—to see the Athletics. But—' he hesitated, —'we lost our return tickets, dropped 'em, or they got stolen, dunno which——' The driver seemed fairly satisfied with this story and Norman thought that, for someone who claimed to be dim, Tony was showing remarkable quickness in making up stories. In fact, it was amazing what old Tony had in him, he thought reflectively.

About an hour later the driver set them down on the A30 and told them in which direction to go for Basingstoke.

'Good luck!' he said, and drove off.

They were all rested. David had been asleep

again and felt rather querulous through being woken up. But he recovered his spirits in the open air. Heather's feet felt better, but as if they were likely to get sore quite quickly again if she walked much.

The sun was going down now, and they were still in a built-up area. Buses went by marked 'Thorpe' and 'Egham' but, as these places weren't on the atlas, it didn't mean anything to the walkers. There were no buses marked 'Basingstoke' and nothing to tell them they were on the right road, until Tony spotted a road sign, which actually said, 'Basingstoke 40 miles'.

'We'll get a lift,' said Norman, 'don't worry.' But he felt very anxious. He was already wondering where they would spend the night. He could see that Heather and David weren't up to walking much further. But where could they sleep?

They didn't get a lift. And there were houses all the way along both sides of the road. Nice houses, set back in pleasant gardens, but no haystacks, nowhere where four children could possibly spend a night out. They had walked only about two or three miles, but it had taken them an hour because Heather and David were going slower and slower, and now it was getting dark. No one would see them in the dark and stop for them, and yet now at last they seemed to be coming to the countryside. Norman felt very disheartened. All this time, and they were really only just out of London. He felt even more bitter about London, sprawling about the way it did, eating up the countryside. Although he was tired and they hadn't got far he felt fiercely determined to get away to Cornwall now. He and Tony could have travelled through the night but Heather and David would have to have a good night's rest. He said to Tony,

'Look out for somewhere to sleep, will you?'

And even as he said it there loomed up through the twilight a wall, and somewhere in the distance behind it a huge strange-looking house.

'Look at that!' said Tony, 'They'd have room to put us up—must be about a fousand rooms in that place, I reckon.'

'They could give us a room each,' said Heather, trying to sound perky.

'Let's knock on the door,' said David, who couldn't sound anything but weary, however hard he tried.

They went along beside the wall, and came to some huge gates and a lodge. Everywhere was in darkness. They stood peering through the gates, then Tony tried one of the side ones—it opened.

'Stone the crows!'

'Look,' said Norman, 'there are huts in the grounds. I bet we could get in one of those, and spend the night.'

He was so relieved at finding somewhere possible that he was almost laughing.

'No fear!' said Tony at once. "That place looks like it's haunted.' He stared up at the huge building with its towers and turrets and hundreds of windows —all in darkness. Heather had shuddered when he said about it being haunted, and had turned away at once. But at the prospect of the road winding on blankly and the dark trees beginning on either side, she suddenly made up her mind, and turned back.

'Nonsense!' she said, firmly. 'No such thing as ghosts, these huts are just being built new in the grounds. I'm sure *they* won't be haunted.'

'That's the style,' said Norman, approvingly. He led the way in, and Heather went next. David followed her, much too tired to be bothered about ghosts. Tony came last, looking all round him distrustfully, but afraid of being left alone outside.

8

HEATHER woke up and heard birds chirping and whistling, and saw that it was light. She felt terribly cramped and her bones ached from lying on the floor after she'd been used to a mattress, lumpy though that had been. She looked over at David and the others. They still seemed to be fast asleep, though Tony had unzipped his side of the sleeping-bag and was sprawling out of it as if he hadn't had enough room. Last night they had spread the polythene bag on the floor of the hut they'd got into (because the window hadn't been made yet), then zipped the two sleeping-bags together to make one double. Then, because it had begun to feel so cold, they'd all squeezed in together. Heather went one end, David next to her, then Norman, and, at the other end, poor Tony, who, being the fattest, had had quite a job getting in at all. They had taken their shoes off and used their anoraks for pillows, and because they were so tired, had slept very comfortably, all things considered. No ghosts had awakened them and the whole place looked a lot less sinister than it had last evening.

Heather wriggled out of the sleeping-bag and in doing so woke the other three. 'It's half past six,' said Norman, 'We'll have breakfast and make an early start. Goodness knows what goes on in these huts in the day time, but there'll be some workmen around I should think.'

'What's for breakfast?' asked Tony.

They all felt rather disappointed when they looked at their stores. They had eaten Tony's cheese sandwiches for supper last night, just before falling asleep. Now all they had left was the boiled ham, four hard-boiled eggs, two packets of crisps, two apples and a smallish piece of fruit cake. None of it seemed suitable for breakfast, but in the end they decided on hard-boiled eggs and apples.

'We'll get some cokes and some more crisps as soon as we get to Basingstoke,' said Tony, who was the treasurer because it was mostly his money anyway.

It didn't take long to eat their breakfast and to get ready to set out on the road again, since no one had to wash or dress. Heather had a small comb in her anorak pocket and she insisted that they all comb their hair so that they wouldn't look too much as if they were on a long journey. Their hands were filthy, but their faces didn't look too bad, and they might find a stream to wash their hands somewhere. She half thought it might have been a good idea to bring some soap, but she didn't really care much and the boys never even thought of it.

They packed up the sleeping-bags and the last

of the food and crept cautiously back up the drive and out through the gates of the huge mansion, feeling like four burglars.

'Crummy!' said Heather, suddenly noticing a large board above the wall, 'Royal Holloway College!'

'Holloway?' said Tony. 'That's a prison, ain't it? We better get going quick!'

They were lucky that morning. They'd only been on the road ten minutes when a lorry picked them up. He was going all the way to Basingstoke and so they just settled down in the cab, rather squashed, to enjoy the ride. This lorry driver was a youngish man. He looked all four of them up and down rather sharply, and Heather wondered if she really looked like a boy. Then the lorry driver glanced at the sleeping-bags.

'You boys been camping?'

'Yes,' said Norman and Tony together.

'Where d'you live?'

'Basingstoke,' they all said at once.

'What part?' said the lorry driver.

Norman felt a horrible sinking feeling in the pit of his stomach, but Tony came to the rescue, after only the tiniest pause,

'Just outside Basingstoke, we lives,' he said. 'Where are you stopping?'

'I'll put you off anywhere you like,' said the lorry driver. 'Where do you want to get off?'

'Well, it's just as you're getting into Basingstoke, you know,' said Tony carefully, then he made an inspired guess, 'Right by that garage.'

'Right by that garage it is, sonny,' said the lorry driver, obligingly.

Norman felt like heaving a sigh of relief. Tony was a marvel. Never again would they pretend they knew the place they were going to, he decided. And they'd have to think up their stories in advance next time. He could hardly wait to get out of the lorry in case the driver asked some more hard questions.

They waved goodbye to the lorry driver at a garage outside Basingstoke, then they walked to the nearest sweet shop and bought some more crisps and four cokes. Norman and Heather went to do the shopping and Heather suggested they should find a greengrocer and get some tomatoes and some more fruit, also a baker's for some bread rolls or something. They did all this, and rejoined the others.

'Whitchurch, Andover, Salisbury,' said Norman, looking at the map. 'Let's find the road and walk for a bit, it's a nice morning.'

On the other side of Basingstoke, they just gloried in being in the country at last. It was wonderful, rolling English country, looking at its best in the early spring. Great fields were touched with yellow where the corn was beginning to come up, and every now and then there was a straight row of trees, showing very dark against the sky.

'Windbreaks,' said Norman, nodding at them.

They found a grassy field and climbed over the gate into it. There they drank their drinks and ate a banana each. Norman had another look at the map.

'Once we get to Andover,' he remarked, 'we could go across country and miss out Salisbury. We could go across by Stonehenge.'

'Wassat?' asked Tony.

The others were horrified.

'Haven't you heard of Stonehenge?' said Heather. 'You're not a lot of credit to the Ancient Britons!'

'Well, I ain't an Ancient Briton, I hope,' retorted Tony, rather bewildered.

They tried to explain what Stonehenge was, and Tony was very keen to see it, so they decided they'd try and get a lift to Andover or Amesbury and have lunch on Salisbury Plain. They thought out a story this time; they would tell whoever gave them a lift that they lived in Basingstoke and were going camping with their uncle, who had arranged to meet them at Stonehenge with the rest of the camping equipment. They felt rather pleased with this story, and soon afterwards, were given a lift to Andover by an elderly lady who had a large old car, with three small dogs in the back.

'In you get,' she said cheerfully, 'if you don't mind the dogs, they won't hurt you!'

Norman grabbed Heather's hand tight so she

wouldn't run away. Tony and David got in first, nearest the dogs, then came Norman, dragging Heather behind.

'Just keep still,' he hissed, 'we won't let them near you.'

The dogs yapped and sniffed around, but Heather soon found out that they were quite harmless. She began to relax. When the lady driver began asking questions they told her their story.

'How exciting!' said the lady, 'and where are you going to camp?'

'Uncle Reg knows the place,' said Tony, ' 'E knows the farmer.' The elderly lady seemed quite satisfied and everyone felt very pleased with themselves. She put them off at Andover on the road to Amesbury, and they set off.

Tony surprised them all. He bounded along with immense enthusiasm and was all for not getting any more lifts but walking the whole of the rest of the way.

'The best holiday I've ever had,' he said, 'I don't care how long it takes us to get there.'

'I don't really,' said Norman, 'but we've got to get there before Mum realizes we're missing and gets worried. Besides, I don't think Heather and David can do too much walking.'

So they got a lift to Amesbury and had lunch in the fields. They told the same story to the man who gave them this lift, but he seemed rather suspicious.

'You mean to say your mothers let you come all the way to Stonehenge without a grown-up, thumbing lifts? And those two young ones with you? I wouldn't let *my* children do that.'

And when he stopped at Amesbury he said,

'Now you be careful who you go asking for lifts another time, there are plenty of bad people about— more than you realize.' He looked very sternly at Norman, who quailed inside,

'Yes, sir, all right, sir,' he said, 'but we'll be with our uncle now so it won't matter.' Then he began to wish that bit were true.

The man had waved his hand and driven off, leaving Norman feeling that he wasn't looking after the others very well. Of course they all knew some judo now, but still they must stick together and be careful. He was very glad that no one realized one of them was a girl. What a good thing Heather had cut her hair off! That man would have been even sterner, if he'd known.

They spent the afternoon and evening tramping across Salisbury Plain, with the sun in their eyes. They stopped for a while at Stonehenge, gazing at it through the National Trust Fence. Tony was the most impressed. He asked question after question about it, till the others realized how little they knew.

'I'll get a book about it,' said Tony, 'when we come to a town.'

But they didn't even get on to the road that night.

They found a hut which didn't have a door, and slept in that—it was on somebody's farm and had been used for storing wood. There were some smelly bits of sacking in it and they spread these under the polythene bag and slept as before.

Heather woke up in the middle of the night and was suddenly horribly homesick for Mum. Through the open door of the hut she could see the moonlight, bright and cold, on the grass. Everything was very, very still. The boys were sound asleep and Heather felt lonely and wanted someone else to be awake and keep her company. Suddenly she realized that they were more than a hundred miles away from Mum and they were completely on their own. She felt terrified and almost leaned over and woke Norman, to tell him she wanted to go back.

'You little silly!' she said to herself, scornfully. 'You'll be perfectly all right in the morning.' She tried hard to think about God and to remember that He cared very much and would look after them. Eventually she dozed off into a rather uncomfortable sleep. When she woke up again she could see it was beginning to get light, and feeling much safer, she fell sound asleep. Norman had to shake her in the end.

'Come on, sleepy-head, we must get on the road. We've got to get to St. Austell by tonight.'

That sounded good to Heather, and she forgot about how far they were from home. Maybe tonight they'd be safe in Nanna's house in St. Austell, being made a fuss of.

Disappointment awaited them when it came to breakfast time, however. They were miles from any shops, and all they had left were two bags of crisps. Nobody had thought of keeping anything for breakfast, the crisps were only left by accident, because they'd been at the bottom of Norman's duffle bag and had been forgotten. They were all very thirsty and crisps weren't much help. So they set off, rather dolefully, keeping the sun behind them and a bit to the left, and hoping they were going in the right direction.

At first, in spite of their hunger and thirst, they weren't too dismal because they all believed they'd come out on a road quite soon and then they'd get a lift. And they were going to try and get a lift to Exeter this time. If they could get a lift all the way to Exeter they could be there by midday and have a pretty good chance of getting the rest of the way by evening, thought Norman. The country was still rolling and grand, but it rolled away on every side with no sign of life or habitation. After London, they'd forgotten that anywhere could be so empty of people and houses. Tony'd never even known. He was amazed and kept saying 'All I want is a coke and then it's marvellous. I'd like to live 'ere, I would.'

Heather had a sore throat and a stiff neck, but she was not going to tell anyone about it. So, in fact, did David, but he was not going to tell anyone either. They both thought they'd be all right if they could just get a drink. Meanwhile, they both kept quiet so as not to make their throats any sorer.

Norman and Tony discussed what tale they should tell the people who were going to give them lifts, to convince them that it was perfectly all right to take four very scruffy and dirty children to Exeter. It was rather a long way, but if only they could get a lift on a long-distance lorry and go all the way in one stretch it would save a lot of time. Thank goodness the weather was holding out, thought Norman, and this looked like being another wonderful day. It had been frosty last night and the hut had had no door. He hoped they'd sleep in St. Austell, warm and cosy tonight.

Tony had another of his bright ideas.

'You know them lay-by places what the lorries pull into when the driver has to get a rest?' Norman nodded.

'I reckon', went on Tony, 'if we could get into the back of one of them, while the driver was having a kip, we'd be laughing.'

'What's "having a kip"?' asked David, his voice sounding very husky.

'Sleeping. He'd never know we was in his lorry, see, and we'd get taken all the way without no explanations.'

'That's a good idea,' said Heather. Her voice was husky too.

'But how do we know where the lorry's going?' asked Norman, 'And how do we get out again without him seeing us?'

'When the lorry stops we jumps down quick on the other side from the driver. I dunno how we knows where it's going though.' He added philosophically—'if it's pointing the right way it's bound to get us a bit further on.'

The sun had gone behind some rather sudden clouds. It had got gloomy and cold all of a sudden. Norman looked at his watch—half-past eight. They must hurry and get on the road. But where was the road?

They were still looking for it an hour later when

it began to rain. The sky was now completely grey and Norman had no idea where the sun was supposed to be. He knew that people who'd lost their sense of direction usually went round in circles and he kept hoping and praying that they'd come upon a road. The countryside seemed to be the same, except that it looked bleak and gloomy now the sun had gone.

The rain came on steadily and Heather sneezed. 'Don't get a cold, me old dear, will you?' said Norman, in his most Cornish voice. She looked so white and miserable.

'My throat hurts,' she whispered.

David still said nothing about his, but a little while later he sneezed too. Norman and Tony looked at him.

'Tell you what,' said Tony, 'if we see a farm it's bound to be on a road, and if we follow the road we'll get to a main road in the end.' No one said anything; they could hardly see through the rain.

'Tell you what,' said Tony, a bit later, 'If we keeps walking downhill we'll get off this blessed plain.' Then he said, 'The rain in Spain falls mainly on the plain. Ha, Ha!'

It was pouring down. Heather felt it dripping off the end of the hood of her anorak, on to her nose, off her nose, on to her chin, and so on. Her plimsolls and her two pairs of socks were soaking. All she could hear was squelch, squelch, squelch, drip, drip,

drip. She looked steadfastly in front of her and kept saying to herself, 'I *know* we were right to come. We *had* to get away. We couldn't stand that place any longer. We're *bound* to reach the road soon.'

They did reach a road in the end. It was quite a good one, but as they came on to it at a right angle they had no idea whether they should go up it or down it. It was half-past eleven. Norman groaned— if only he had a compass. Tony suggested that they toss up. Heads they'd go left, tails they'd go right. It was tails, so off they went.

'The first car we sees, we'll stop,' said Tony. 'Or the first house we sees we'll knock at the door. We'll say we're on a geography expedition from school and we've dropped our compass and got to get back to—um—what's the most likeliest town?'

Norman pulled the atlas out of the front of his anorak where he always kept it handy. 'Better not say Exeter—better say Yeovil or Ilchester, they're nearer. Gillingham's the only other place marked here. And we may have passed that, for all we know. Don't want to go backwards.'

'I'll say the road to Yeovil or Ilchester,' said Tony. 'We can pretend we got instructions to go in that direction.'

Norman looked at him admiringly, and wondered what he'd have done without Tony's powers of invention. He'd always been brought up to tell the truth and be honest, so that he couldn't for the life of him make up things so quickly the way Tony did. He knew it was wrong really, but neither could he see what else they could do.

Heather thought all this, but she couldn't say it because her throat felt as if it had swelled all up inside and got covered with fur. Her nose tickled and she kept sneezing. Her head ached, in fact she ached all over, and just longed to sit down. Then David, who was in much the same state as Heather, spotted a house.

'House!' he shouted, forgetting his voice, which croaked and broke. Norman went to the door and did the asking. He hoped the woman would not realize that his voice was Cornish, and not some other part of Wiltshire. The others stayed outside in the road, for they were now getting worried in case they didn't reach St. Austell that night. A search would probably begin for them the next day when they didn't return from Grandad Parker's. Norman came back to them full of relief.

'Just a bit further down this road, the way we're going, and we'll come to the junction with the main road to Ilchester. Turn left and we'll be heading towards Ilchester. She says Ilchester's an awful long way, but I said we only wanted the Ilchester road.'

They trudged off.

'Oh!' said Heather, after a minute, 'I wish we'd asked for a glass of water!'

'Never mind,' said Tony, 'there'll be another

house soon.' But there wasn't. They did come to a lay-by, and there, parked in it, was a great green tarpaulin-covered lorry. Their hopes rose. They sunk again after David, being the smallest, and least likely to be seen, had crept up and examined the lorry.

'It's a great big load, and it's all tied down, ever so strongly,' he croaked. 'There's no room at all for any of us, and the driver's asleep in the cab.'

Tony went to check and see if this were true and there was no hope at all of stealing a ride unseen. Just as he got up to the lorry the engine began to rev. The driver was starting up, and before Tony had time to run round to the front to beg a lift, the lorry had moved off into the road again and was soon roaring away down the road towards Ilchester.

'I vote,' said Norman, 'that we stop here for a bit and see if another lorry comes that we *can* get on. Maybe two of us could go down the road a little way just in case there's a house we could get a drink from.' But they decided against splitting up in case they missed their chance of a lift. They all squatted down on the other side of the hedge, so that they would not be seen by anyone driving into the lay-by. They spread the polythene bag out as a sort of tent, and told each other stories and ate the crisps. At least, Norman and Tony ate the crisps, Heather kept sticking her tongue out to catch the rain drops. And Norman and Tony told funny stories.

Then after about half an hour, when they were

beginning to think that no more lorries were going to pull in, they heard the sound of a heavy engine slowing down and stopping, just the other side of the hedge. They peered through. It was one of those big, covered lorries, and the driver was climbing out. He walked down to the end of the lay-by and climbed over the gate into the field, then he eventually disappeared among some trees.

'Quick,' whispered Norman, almost as soon as he was over the gate. 'David, pop out and see if the back's empty, and if there's room for us.' David did, and then beckoned frantically. He could hardly speak now. The others tumbled through a hole in the hedge. Thank goodness! The whole of the back of the lorry was empty. There was only one snag: there was a hole through which the driver could glance back to see if everything was all right behind. They climbed up into the lorry and lay down on the right hand side, the side the driver couldn't see when he glanced back.

'Just pray he doesn't come and look in before he starts off again,' said Tony.

'He hasn't got a load. Nothing to check,' said Norman, but his heart was beating madly.

It was just as well they'd been quick, for the driver came back almost at once and started up. He didn't look in the back—after all, as far as he knew there wasn't a living soul for miles around . . .

9

NORMAN woke up with a jolt, and rolled over against Tony, then he remembered with a feeling of panic where they were. He heard the door of the driver's cab slam, and lay hardly breathing, waiting for someone to catch them and haul them off to the police station. But nothing happened. Cautiously he sat up, and saw that Tony was doing the same. His round blue eyes were blinking the sleep out of them.

'Stone the crows! We been asleep. Wasser time?'

'Six-thirty,' said Norman, feeling rather funny. 'Where on earth are we?'

'Better go and have a dekko.'

Heather and David were rubbing their eyes and sitting up when he came back.

'We're at a caff. There are a lot of lorries and a lot of men sitting round smoking. I reckon we could get some cokes in there.'

This suggestion was most welcome, and Tony went off with the utmost confidence to get four cokes. They decided they'd better get out of the lorry and find out where they were somehow. So they got out, stretching and yawning, but feeling much better, apart from the colds, which were worse. Heather didn't have such a headache, but her nose had begun to drip.

It had stopped raining, and they sat down on a wall a bit further on from the 'caff' to wait for Tony. When he came, he was looking rather as if he'd seen a ghost.

'Get behind the wall,' he gasped. 'Don't want to be seen, do you? It's on the wireless about you. I just heard it, didn't I? I goes in to get four cokes and I'm just coming out again and I goes back and asks if she got anything for a cold—and blow me down—the next minute the chap on the radio says "Three children reported missing from their home in South-East London since Monday, believed to be making for Cornwall". Then he says your names—Norman, Evver and David Pendray—then he starts to say what clothes you got on—I didn't stop to hear no more. I says "thanks very much" and comes out with me cokes.'

'That'll look suspicious,' said Norman.

'Yes, I know,' said Tony, 'but I was buying four cokes, and I just got scared, didn't I? They might've said something about *me* next.'

Well, said Norman, 'we'd better not be seen together any more. If we go along in twos, it won't be so noticeable. And they don't know Heather's not a boy.' He said it rather dolefully, though. He even thought it'd be better if they gave themselves up right away, but he didn't say so, because Heather said,

'Well, we've come a long way, and we're going to finish it, they're going to have a nasty time if they try and catch me now.' And she looked fierce and determined, quite her old self again.

'I votes we gets in that lorry again, if we can,' said Tony. 'Nobody's going to give us a lift any more, that's for sure. So we might as well go with the lorry until we finds out where we are.'

This was agreed upon, and so, in twos, Norman with Heather, and Tony with David, they went back to the 'caff', coming from different directions, and found to their relief that their lorry was still there. They got back up in the right hand corner, but not to sleep this time. They huddled together silently, looking out of the back of the lorry waiting to see some hostile face, glaring in and challenging them.

But in a quarter of an hour, the lorry rumbled off. It was dry now, but dull, so that it seemed to get dark earlier and it was difficult to tell where they were from the dark corner they were forced to stay in. Then lights began and they realized they were coming into a town. Norman went wriggling on his stomach down to the open end of the lorry to see if he could spot a place name. It was a town of some kind but they weren't in a shopping area and he couldn't see the road signs pointing to the road he was travelling on. So it wasn't much use. They rumbled on for hours, they could be anywhere, he realized, absolutely anywhere. The lorry could have taken a north-west direction and be going up to Taunton, Bridgwater, Bristol. They might even be in Wales, for all he knew.

And then, hours later, the lorry pulled up again. They were in another lay-by and the driver seemed to be going to sleep. After about ten minutes of lying still and quiet, David began to make known to the others his need to get out. In the end he gave up and just wriggled along to the back of the lorry and climbed out. The others, of course, had to follow.

They found they were on quite high ground, and downhill a little way they saw some lights. They began to wander towards them, keeping close together on the rough grass. The moon kept coming out, and then sidling behind lumps of cloud again.

Heather heard a sort of snuffle, and looked behind her. Then she gave a stifled scream, grabbed Tony and began to run. Tony looked when she screamed, and saw a great dark shape behind them. He panicked and ran too.

Actually, it was just a cow, which had come to see its 'visitors'. But Heather and Tony'd stumbled quite a way down the hill before Norman and David could catch them up to explain. Then they all sat down on the ground and couldn't stop giggling.

It was then—far off—that they heard it. They stopped giggling at once and jumped up. They even hurried up the hill again. But of course it was too late. By the time they'd reached the road, it was empty. And somewhere far away in the blackness they could still hear the sound of the engine droning faintly into the night air.

Tony shrugged philosophically:

'Well, that's it, ain't it?'

'Let's walk,' said Heather, 'I feel like walking. I'd had about enough of that lorry anyway.'

They all agreed and marched off briskly in the direction the lorry had been pointing when it stopped. After about half an hour they found a village in darkness, then a cross-roads and—at last— a sign-post. The road they were on said 'B3212 Dartmoor'. Tony could not have been more pleased.

'Dartmoor!' he said, in ecstasy, 'Where all them criminals escape from! I didn't fink we was coming near here.'

Norman felt a tremendous relief to know that they were still on the right road.

'I wish we'd stayed on that lorry, though,' he said, 'It might have taken us right across Dartmoor.'

'Coo, I'm glad we didn't,' said Tony. 'Now we can walk right past the prison!'

Norman did wonder whether they should take the other road—which said 'A382 Okehampton' on it. But it looked as if that was a longer way round. And besides, they would be caught more easily on the main road. They were 'wanted' now, so maybe Dartmoor, with all its terrors, was the place for them.

He led the way up the smaller, winding road. Tony, in his townsman's ignorance, didn't know about the bogs or the sudden mists. Still, if they kept on the road they were bound to be all right . . .

It was uphill all the way, and they climbed for hours. They heard sheep bleating away from them, and sometimes galloping hoofs of startled ponies, and all the time up and up they went. There were no houses, nowhere to shelter. About one o'clock in the morning they found a hollow beside the road, spread out the ground-sheet and the sleeping bags, and lay down, very high up under the stars.

It was very cold and they were all feeling extremely empty inside, so none of them got to sleep. After about an hour they decided to walk again. The moon had come out properly now, and they could see the white road stretching ahead, and the moor and the granite crags spread out all around them. It was so still and desolate that they clutched one another as they walked along. They didn't feel like talking. There seemed to be listeners all round in the empty moonlit air. They were much more frightened than they'd been in the 'haunted' house. Norman found he kept on thinking of spooky stories he'd heard about Dartmoor—he kept remembering the story of Bengie, the lost spirit of one of the Mayors of Okehampton, who'd been condemned to empty the waters of a pool with a sieve. You could hear his groans as he laboured, night after night, and the gurgle of the water as it ran out of the sieve.

Horrors! What if they should meet Bengie? He looked round fearfully and caught David taking a stealthy look round too. Oh dear! It was no good frightening the younger ones. He grinned at David and said as loudly as he dared,

'Tired, old soul? Not much further to go, we'll be in Cornwall tomorrow morning.'

'I'm not tired,' said David stoutly, 'I was just thinking though—it's a bit spooky up here.'

'Rubbish!' said the other three very loudly.

They walked on a bit in silence, then a voice inside Norman's brain said 'Bengie!' He went cold all over, and told himself to stop thinking about it. 'Shut up, you fool!' he said to himself. But a moment later he thought it again, and he kept wanting to look round and see if anyone was behind them. He looked round—and this time caught Heather looking round too. In another minute, he thought, we'll all panic and start running and perhaps run off the road and get lost.

'Let's sing "Onward, Christian Soldiers",' he said.

So they began—singing quietly so as not to attract attention. But the moor was so quiet and still all round that they petered out after a bit.

'Don't let's sing,' said Tony, 'I feel as if there's somebody listening when we make a noise.'

'There *is* someone listening,' said Heather. The

others jumped.

'Oo-er!' said David, in a wobbly voice.

'Don't be silly, Heather!' snapped Norman.

'I'm not,' croaked Heather, offended, 'I mean God. He's listening.'

Norman felt relieved. He decided that, if those silly thoughts came back, he would say the Lord's Prayer through to himself, and anything else he could remember out of the Bible and that would keep them out.

Tony also felt a lot less eerie at the mention of God's Name. After all, he thought, if there were listeners, they might be good ones—or there might be just one Big Listener who was good. He felt like starting a friendly argument to cheer everyone up: 'How do you know there's a God?' he began, just to start things off and get everyone talking. He was surprised that Heather got so snappy about it.

'Course there's a God,' she croaked. '*Isn't* there, Norman?'

'Yes,' said Norman, '*I* believe it.' But, as he said it, he wondered, and got terribly afraid and worried. How he wished they were safely in St. Austell! Would they ever get over Dartmoor? And if they did, would they ever get to St. Austell without getting caught? And why had they come anyway? Why had they run away from everything? In the morning I'll feel different, he said to himself.

'Yes, but how do you *know*?' persisted Tony.

'The Bible's all about Him,' said Heather, 'and I *know* it's true. If you belong to Him you know He's there. And He'll help you through *anything*, if you . . . ' Her voice faltered. Not because of her sore throat. Suddenly she saw that they were running away because Trefoil Street and the Sterks had been too much for them. And she had promised Him that she would be on His side . . . It was as if Tony read her thoughts.

'Help you through *anything*? What you all running away for, then?'

Nobody answered. Then David said:

'Can we have a sit-down now, please, Norman?' and he sounded so weary and miserable that they at once forgot the discussion, and felt worn out too. They didn't even look for a sheltered place—just huddled together on the polythene bag and tucked the sleeping bags all round themselves, and in no time they were all asleep.

Heather awoke a few hours later, and found it was early morning, and that the sun was going to come up soon, judging by the whiteness over at one end of the sky. Across the road the moor sloped upwards and at the top was an outcrop of gaunt rocks. She decided to climb them to see if they were near the end of the moor. Or perhaps she might see a farmhouse where they could beg a drink of water, or even milk. She'd stopped feeling hungry now but the back of her nose was tight, hot and snuffly, and her throat was still lined with sandpaper. She wriggled out of her bit of sleeping-bag, stretched a bit, and went towards the rock.

Her legs ached, but she scrambled up and sat on top of it. All around her was the moor, bleak and desolate, brown in some parts, black in others. The sun began to come up and she turned eastwards to get the warmth on her cold face. And as she did so she remembered Mum again. Mum! They'd left her to face London on her own. And now Mum knew they'd gone, but didn't know what had happened to them. She wanted to call out:

'It's all right, Mum, we're nearly there. Don't worry about us.' She remembered when the accident had happened to Dad—Mum holding her tight, and saying 'God will take care of us', over and over again through her tears. Mum needed her and Norman and David! How could they ever have run away and left her? Run away! With that thought another memory came into her mind. Mr. Lane's voice this time,

'He wasn't afraid of the worst places on earth . . . His friends were terrified . . . but *He* didn't run away . . . '

Jesus had stayed right through to the bitter end, Heather thought, and then He had been triumphant. She had asked to be on His side because He was great and strong and noble. And at the first bit of unpleasantness she had deserted and brought the others with her.

She sat on the rock, staring dumbly towards the east, her throat aching with misery, and the thoughts pouring in at her. A dog—even a mad dog—wasn't enough to run away from. Perched up on the immense moor, she saw—too late—that it was too small a thing. They'd come hundreds of miles, they'd walked through the night on to Dartmoor. If God could protect them through all that, He wouldn't let a *dog* hurt them . . .

She went on sitting, shaking with cold, staring at the bright east—beaten at last.

Norman had watched her go away towards the rock. He hadn't slept as well as the others, for the simple reason that he was suddenly desperately anxious to get to St. Austell and get the whole business over and done with. He was tensed, rigid with worry under the sleeping-bag. If only they could get to St. Austell today, and send a message to Mum to tell her they were safe. He was in charge. He would get all the blame if anything happened . . .

Tony awoke and groaned:

'I'm starving. We ain't got no food, have we?'

Norman shook his head:

'We should be able to find a spring up here,' he said. 'When we come to Princetown we might be able to buy some food if we dare go and ask for it.'

They woke David and packed up the sleeping-bags. David was very white and quiet. Heather had seen their movement and was coming back. It couldn't be long now. Soon they'd be in Cornwall.

'See anyfink from up there, Evver?' inquired Tony.

'No,' she said listlessly, 'it goes on for ever.'

'Rubbish,' said Norman emphatically. 'Come on —let's get going. The sooner we start, the sooner we'll get to St. Austell.'

'I'm going back,' said Heather.

The boys stared at her as if she were delirious.

'I was wrong to come,' she said through her chattering teeth, 'I'm going back. Mum needs us.'

'But we're nearly there!' said Tony.

'I'm not going all that way back,' said David in a wail.

'We must. We must give ourselves up. The police'll take us back to London,' said Heather, sadly, 'we won't have to walk it.'

'But we might as well go on now,' said Tony, 'No sense in turning round—what d'you say, Norm?'

Norman said slowly:

'If they found out about us yesterday and put it on the wireless and everything, Mum must be terribly worried.'

'She probably thinks we've been killed,' said Heather.

'Yes, we'll go back,' said Norman, at that, 'we must.'

It was two against two. David was feeling so ill he couldn't argue any more. Tony knew *he* would have to go back to London in any case. He shrugged his shoulders high up and down to show what he thought. Then he turned round and set off the way they had come. Pity he hadn't seen Cornwall, he thought. Never mind, he'd do it again one day.

The other three followed, dragging along. They had turned their backs on Cornwall for good, thought Heather tragically. She knew she was right, but the thought that they were nearly there made her cry with disappointment. She turned her face away from the boys so they wouldn't notice the tears rolling down. Norman did notice, but he knew it was best not to say anything.

'Poor old Hairpin,' he thought. He himself felt as if a great load were off his back. And now they were doing the right thing surely they deserved some help.

'Please God,' he asked silently, 'will You send us something to give us a lift to the nearest police-station? David needs it.' He kept looking round to see if anything were coming their way, but the road was as quiet as ever. Up in the pale blue sky a hawk hovered. Down a heather-covered slope, a group of shaggy ponies took fright at the children and thundered off.

The moor had been white with hoar-frost. Now the sun was changing it back to purple. They all got warmer as they walked.

'Heather,' said Norman suddenly, 'why not take some heather back to London?'

He said it to cheer her up, but was astonished at the effect his words had on Tony. Tony had never realized that Heather's name was really a flower. At first he thought Norman was talking nonsense, but when he saw Heather tugging at the wiry stems of the purple flowers all around them he got very excited.

'Cor,' he said, 'this trip's educational, ain't it? We ought to be paid for doing it.'

He helped Heather pick with such enthusiasm that the other two joined in and soon she had a great armful. They all cheered up in the process.

And then they heard the hum of a powerful engine somewhere in the distance. It reminded them of what they had to do.

'Quick! Get ready!' said Norman.

They spread out down the side of the road, facing east, swinging their thumbs. Then, as the sound got nearer, they realized with a funny sort of disappointment that the car was on the road in front of them. It was heading over Dartmoor, towards Cornwall. They all hesitated, and then they all looked at Heather, without saying anything.

She wavered. Should she turn round again? Should they jump across the road and go on with the journey, on to Cornwall? She looked at Norman.

And then the car shot into view, and began to slow down. It was a big black car with a blue lamp.

Tony was the only one who wasn't speechless, and he could only find two words to utter.

'Crumbs!' he said, 'Cops!'

10

It was two weeks later. It was in Trefoil Street and Rachel had come to tea, with three very brown and healthy-looking Pendrays. After tea Mrs. Pendray had gone to watch T.V. with Mr. and Mrs. Forrest, and Tony had come next door to help David with a model of a Mustang that David had just had for his birthday. Norman had gone to post a letter to Nanna Pendray.

Rachel was hearing all about the journey to Cornwall.

'You lot have all the fun,' she said enviously, 'I wish I could've come too.'

'It wouldn't have been fun—it would have been dismal—if we hadn't had that holiday in Cornwall on the end of it,' said Heather.

'It was great of them cops,' said Tony. 'They said they'd take us on to St. Austell so Evver's grannie could decide what to do wiv us.'

'And she decided you could stay and have a holiday with her?'

'Yes. Said we looked as if we needed it. But the best bit was stopping off in that prison.'

'Stopping off in prison?' said Rachel, bewildered. It didn't sound very good.

'That really made his day,' said Heather. 'The policemen that picked us up, took us to Dartmoor prison—they radioed to London from there——' she added, laughing at the expression on Rachel's face, 'and then a London policeman came here to tell Mum not to worry, they'd found us.'

'Told *my* mum an' all,' said Tony, 'only she fought I was at the camp down in Kent, so she nearly had a fit. We had breakfast in Dartmoor prison,' he added nonchalantly.

'But we didn't see any convicts,' said David, 'I hoped we would, didn't you, Tony? It was a good prison though, wasn't it? I wonder if it's better than the Tower of London?'

'Piles better,' said Tony, in the manner of an expert, 'and piles better too than that 'Olloway where we stopped the night. I don't fink much of their security.'

'I keep telling you,' said Heather, 'it wasn't a prison, it was a College. It said so. That's why it was empty—all the students were away for Easter.'

'Well the only 'Olloway *I've* heard of is a prison,' grunted Tony and went back to the Mustang.

'Oh,' sighed Rachel again, 'what a lot of exciting things happened to you. Were you ever afraid?'

'Not much,' said Heather. Then she glanced over at the boys, and leaned towards Rachel:

'Norman says he'd been praying for a lift when that police-car came. Do things happen like that?'

'Why not?' said Rachel softly. 'It was what he was wanting, wasn't it?'

'Only it was going the other way,' said Heather.

'All the better,' said Rachel, 'I'd say that was very kind of God.'

'Yes,' said Heather slowly. 'Yes—p'raps that's right. It was the very best thing—we saw Cornwall after all, and Mum was told ever so quickly so she stopped worrying . . . and then when Nanna said we needed fattening up and could stay if Mum would agree . . . as if Tony Forrest needed fattening,' she added more loudly.

'I 'eard that! I lost a lot of weight on that trip. I was getting like a 'Airpin, I was.'

'Well, you put it all on again at Nanna's. Only listen to this, Rachel—he wouldn't touch the Cornish cream. Said he'd rather have ideal milk!'

'You watch it, young Evver, or we'll gag you, won't we, David?'

'You bet!' said David eagerly.

Then Norman came in.

'I got news for you lot,' he said grinning, 'and especially for you Heather. Sterks's dog's been destroyed. Police took it away 'cos it bit the postman. Who said they always win?'

'They can't win,' said David, stoutly, 'I'm glad we came back.'

Heather thought of Mum's beaming face at the station the day before. She hadn't told them off, not one word. Instead she'd said *she* was sorry because she'd been so busy with her job, and trying to find somewhere nicer to live, that she hadn't noticed how much the children hated it. But they were to spend the whole of the summer holidays with Nanna Pendray if she'd have them. And she'd been talking to Heather's teacher, and he thought she could try for a place at Rachel's school next year if she worked hard.

'Yes, I'm glad too,' said Heather.

'And me,' said Norman.

'Tell you what, though, said Tony, flying the half-finished plane around in the air as he spoke, 'Here's somefink *you* don't know. The rest of Trefoil Street's being pulled down in August. Our landlord sent my dad the notice this morning. We'll all be put in posh new flats, I expect.' He put the plane down and unwrapped a fresh piece of pink gum to celebrate.

Heather tried to picture Trefoil Street not there, and couldn't. She kept seeing Conrad and Inez, who'd tried hard to keep the Watch Committee going even when the Pendrays had run away, and the mums and dads who'd made a welcome crowd in the street when they'd come back to show them that they were glad. They'd appreciated the Watch Committee! Trefoil Street wasn't such a bad street after all.

'Well,' she said, rather surprised at herself, 'I'm

a bit sorry in a way. We're just settling down.'

' 'Ere,' said Tony, 'would you like me to sing 'Ome Sweet 'Ome for you?'

'For goodness' sake!' protested Norman. (He had heard Tony's singing before.)

'Well, you watch it, young Evver,' warned Tony, 'or I will—and it'll be worse than anyfink you've suffered yet.' He threw a large wrapped square of gum at her.

'Stick that in your cake-hole and stop your grumbling.'